SO YOU HAVE MY SECRET BABY

SO YOU WANT TO BE A BILLIONAIRE BOOK 4

ELIZABETH MADDREY

1

Holly Bell checked the clock at the bottom of her monitor. Almost five. Luca's sitter was okay with making dinner tonight, which was a huge blessing, but Holly still wanted to get home in time to put her baby to bed.

Not that he was a baby. He'd be the first to tell you that, too. Indignantly. Luca was a newly-minted nine, half-way through the third grade, and as far as he was concerned, ready to be the man of the house.

Holly's lips twitched. Well, she wasn't going to be ceding authority to him any time soon, but she didn't miss the hardship of having an infant. Not that nine didn't come with troubles of its own.

"Knock knock?"

Holly swiveled in her chair and her eyebrows lifted as her gaze landed on the oh-so-handsome-but-out-of-her-league Aaron Powell. "Hi."

"Heya. Do you have some time that we could chat? Figured we should coordinate our schedules and get ready to take on this contest, you know? Even though we're ultimately competing against one another, for now Tyler was pretty clear that we needed to act like a team."

Holly nodded. Tyler had actually said they needed to *be* a team, but maybe acting like one was as close as Aaron could get. "I have a few minutes. I can't stay late tonight, I'm sorry. When I know in advance, it's not a problem to adjust my hours, but short notice is hard."

Aaron sent her an expectant look.

Well, let him. She didn't see the need to offer more details than that. If he asked, she'd think about it, but Luca wasn't someone she paraded around. In fact, it was probable there were plenty of coworkers who didn't realize she was a single mom. She liked it that way. She'd prefer to keep it that way. "Why don't you take a seat? Did you bring your calendar?"

Aaron pulled a phone out of his pocket as he moved to the chair she had wedged in the corner of her cube and sat. "Everything's on here. This baby's my life."

"Ah." Holly reached for the spiral-bound planner she kept open beside her keyboard and a pen. "I can't do electronic. I've tried them all."

He frowned. "But how will we work together?"

"Email? Shared apps?" She shrugged. She did plenty of working in teams as part of her job. She was a programmer in the social media division of Robinson Enterprises. She was perfectly capable of using all the electronic tools anyone could possibly want. She just happened to prefer to keep her calendar on paper.

"Yeah, I was thinking a shared calendar."

"That's fine. Set it up and invite me. I'll transfer to my planner and back as needed."

"That seems . . . inefficient."

She shrugged again. "Not your problem though, right?"

"I guess not." Aaron sighed. "The first deliverable is a five-year plan. I was thinking we could just split it up and then get together to merge our thoughts into one."

Holly bit her lip. "You think that's okay? There was a lot of synergy talk in there."

Aaron chuckled. "Sure, but it's not like divide and conquer is a strange concept. You really think they want us wasting billable hours sitting in the same room and typing on one machine while the other person looks on? That's dumb."

"Okay. Although they did say it was fine to work on it during office hours, provided our other work got done." It would be easier for her, certainly, not to have to do it that way. Then she could work at home while Luca was playing on his Nintendo Switch or after he went to bed. "I scanned the template. Do you want to do first half and second half or something else?"

"What about evens and odds?"

Holly thought over what she remembered of the business plan template and nodded. "Sure, that works. Do you have a preference?"

"I can take the odds." Aaron swiped at his phone. "Then what if we got together on Wednesday at, say, three to go over what we have and start merging?"

Holly glanced at her schedule for Wednesday. "I have a meeting that ends at three on Wednesday. It's usually over on time, but not always. What if we said three thirty, just in case?"

"Yeah, that works. Do you mind coming to my office? I didn't realize you were over here in the programmer bullpen."

Holly laughed. "No one calls it that but you guys."

"Who do you mean?" He bristled.

"The customer experience managers—you guys. Although actually, maybe the user interface folks get on the bullpen kick every now and then. But the programmers? We don't actually understand why. These are cubes, same as on every floor of this building, not some open concept cop shop."

Aaron snorted. "I'll make a note."

She smiled. "Maybe you could mention it at your next bigwig meeting."

"Sure." He shook his head. "But back to the question—my office is okay?"

"Oh, yeah, that's fine. Nicer not to risk everyone hanging on your words." She snapped her mouth shut. That had come out a little snippier than she'd intended. But she was getting a little flack from the guys on her row about having been chosen to compete to run this arm of the company. She did good work. Her record, obviously, stood on its own. But there were programmers who were better at coding—no question there. In her opinion, the guys she could think of who fit that bill lacked what she'd call the soft skills necessary to hold a management position. Maybe Joe Robinson, the company owner, had noticed that as well, and that was why she'd been chosen to go up against Aaron.

Holly might not have a chance to win, but she was sure going to give it her best shot.

She'd gotten a double major in business and computer science, so it wasn't as if she didn't know things beyond coding.

"Great. So, three thirty on Wednesday. Then, we're supposed to send it to Tyler to look over on Friday—so he can make sure we're on the right track. Think we should meet again before that? I could do eight Friday morning." Aaron looked up from his phone. "Does that work?"

"Sure." Holly wrote both meetings in her book, adding a mental note that she'd need to plan for before-school care for Luca on Friday. That was an easy enough sell—Luca loved getting dropped off early so he could hang out with his friends before class. "Do you want to schedule some standing meeting times? We're going to have lots of deliverables over the next six months. It's not unreasonable to have time set aside."

"Smart. The Wednesday time would work for me. As would the Friday." Aaron glanced up and met her gaze. "What about you?"

Holly caught her lip between her teeth. "I don't normally get in until nine. Would that work?"

"Yeah, I guess. You can't just shift your schedule?"

"Not easily. I'll do it if I have to, but I'd like to avoid it if I can." She made good money at her job, but her budget was still a careful balancing act. Adding in before-school care every week? That would take more juggling than she wanted to deal with.

"Okay. We'll give it a shot." Aaron tapped on his phone. "There. I sent you a link to the calendar. It'd be easier if we were both using it."

"We will be." She sent him a toothy smile. Lots of people gave her a hard time about her paper planner. Whatever. She didn't miss meetings or deadlines, so they could deal.

He shook his head as he stood. "Okay. Well. I guess I'll see you Wednesday."

"Yep. See ya." Holly spun back to her monitor. She'd admired Aaron Powell from a distance—he was easy on the eyes—but she hadn't had many opportunities to interact with him. It would be interesting to get to know him in the coming months. She glanced at the clock. She could probably squeeze another twenty minutes of work before she needed to get home. That was probably enough time to chase down why the module Trent was in charge of wasn't compiling.

AARON MUTTERED to himself all the way from Holly's cube to his office. How had she ended up as his teammate-slash-competitor? He could think of about twelve people, and that was just off the top of his head, who would be a better choice than someone like Holly Bell. He didn't even *know* her and it was obvious she wasn't committed to the company.

All the teams were a guy and a girl. So okay, that knocked his twelve to four—maybe five. And still. What did a programmer have to offer in the overall scheme of things? Oh, sure, Social needed the coders. They were the backbone. But they did their job, stayed in the background, and avoided the spotlight.

So what was Holly Bell's story?

And why couldn't she come in early on Fridays to make his life easier?

Nine. He rolled his eyes as he strode into his office. At least he'd have some work done by then, but how did she expect to win this competition if she wasn't going to put in the work? Flip side? He had this in the bag.

Maybe he ought to let Tyler know he appreciated the gimme.

Nah. That was obnoxious. He wasn't that guy anymore. Or at least he was trying not to be.

Speaking of which, he'd better get a move on if he wasn't going to be late for Bible study. Was it Christopher's night for dinner this week? Hopefully. Aaron was in the mood for fried chicken and all the sides.

He packed up his laptop and a handful of files that he wanted to spend a few minutes looking at tonight if he had time. If he didn't? No big deal to just bring them back with him again in the morning.

"Night, Ella." Aaron nodded to the admin-slash-office manager who sat at the desk facing the elevator lobby.

"Night, Aaron. Oh, heard you got picked for the competition. Congrats. And good luck."

He flashed a smile. "Thanks. You have any scoop on Holly Bell?"

"Now, Aaron, you know I don't gossip."

"Uh-huh." Aaron scooted closer to her desk.

Ella glanced around. "There's not a lot to say. She's quiet. Does good work. Everyone likes her. And she's regular as clockwork when it comes to her hours. In at nine, out at five thirty. Six on the rare, off day."

"Eight hours plus lunch, huh?" That didn't seem like the kind of employee Joe would choose as a candidate for Senior Vice President in charge of a division. There had to be more to her, didn't there? "Anything else?"

"Not really. She's sweet. Always says hi. Brings cookies sometimes. And on sunny days, she eats her lunch out on the terrace off six and reads."

Aaron nodded. The terrace garden on the sixth floor was a nice place to grab a few minutes of downtime. Lots of people ate their lunch out there. "What's she read?"

Ella shook her head. "Not sure. Usually on her phone, so it could be anything. You'll be getting to know her. You can ask."

He laughed. "Oh, yeah, I'll get right on that. I doubt very much we're going to be bonding over books."

"You never know. It could happen." Ella grinned and leaned forward. Aaron kept his gaze steady on her face. Ella was a nice, older lady, but she liked to try and trap guys into looking at her cleavage. Why? No one knew. She was, by all accounts, happily married. Maybe she just liked the attention. "I know you read— I've seen you doing it."

"Guilty. But I still don't think Holly's going to turn out to be a lover of epic fantasy."

"Stranger things have happened. She's a programmer, after all."

He nodded, acknowledging her point. "I guess we'll see. Have a good night, Ella."

"You, too. Bible study night, right?"

"You got it." He waved and pushed through the glass doors

that led out to the elevators. Had he learned anything about Holly he didn't already know? Nope. But maybe that was information of its own. Maybe Holly was exactly what she looked like —a steady, solidly average worker bee.

And none of that helped him understand why Joe had chosen her for this competition.

He crowded onto an elevator with a bunch of others who were all calling it a night. There was chatter—generic chit-chat between people who knew each other, making plans for the next day or the weekend—but Aaron tried to ignore it.

There was a time when he would have had his ear to the ground, in case someone mentioned a party. Then he would've wrangled an invitation.

He wasn't that guy anymore.

It didn't mean the temptation wasn't still there.

In the garage, he waited for his turn to exit the elevator and headed through the parked cars to the far side of the lot where he'd angled his sports car across two spots to minimize the chances of anyone dinging the doors. Or worse. He got looks, sometimes, but there were plenty of spaces.

He unlocked the driver's side door, tossed his laptop bag into the passenger seat, and slid behind the wheel.

It wasn't far to the condo where the men's Bible study met. It was a good group of guys from work. Aaron frowned—were they all part of the contest? They were. Huh. What were the odds?

He found a parking spot and made his way up to the condo Christopher Ward and Ryan Foster shared. He hit the buzzer for the door. He was a few minutes early, but not too many.

The door opened and Ryan grinned at him. "Hey, man. Glad you could make it. Come on in. Chris is unloading the chicken."

Aaron laughed. "Knew it."

"Right?" Ryan chuckled and led the way.

Aaron made sure the door was shut behind him before heading to the kitchen.

"It's always bucket chicken when you're in charge, man. Why is that?" Aaron reached for a fry, stopping when Ryan laughed. "What?"

"Nothing. That sounds like Ian." Ryan turned and left the kitchen.

Christopher pointed to the stack of plates. "If you're going to eat, why not do it properly."

"Yes, ma'am." Aaron smirked as he reached for a plate and started loading it.

"Chicken night." Ian came into the kitchen rubbing his hands together. "I've been looking forward to this all weekend."

"It might not have been chicken." Christopher stepped away from the island to make room for the others to fill their plates. He crossed his arms. "Sometimes I cook."

The banter continued as the guys filled their plates and ate. After the food was gone, they settled in for the lesson from Mark chapter eight.

What does it profit a man to gain the whole world but lose his soul?

Aaron frowned as the words echoed in his head. They were featured in a lot of Christian music. And sermons that cautioned against greed and seeking after money. And he got it—the whole notion that someone couldn't serve God and money made absolute sense to him. He'd done his share of chasing money, power, and prestige in college and right after. At the time, he would have said he was living the high life. Looking back?

He'd never felt emptier.

Jesus had changed all that. Thankfully.

Was this competition going to be too much temptation to slide back into his old way of thinking? He'd keep it in mind—he'd pray about it. A lot.

Maybe now that he had Jesus in his life, and he had his priorities straight, a position of authority and the money that came with it wouldn't be something that derailed his Christian walk. Joe Robinson was a believer—and a billionaire—so surely the two things weren't completely incompatible.

2

Aaron frowned at the clock. They'd agreed on eight a.m., hadn't they? Holly had balked at making Fridays at eight the standing time, but she'd still agreed to meet for this one. Or, at least, that was how he'd perceived her comments. If it had changed, why wouldn't she have said something?

"Sorry. I know I'm late." Holly bustled into his office, still wearing her coat and carrying the enormous laptop bag he'd often seen her with at the elevators.

His eyebrows lifted. "I was starting to wonder."

"I know." She blew a tuft of hair out of her eyes and set her insulated mug down on the round table he had in the corner for small meetings. Holly unwound her scarf, shrugged out of her jacket, and pulled out a chair. "Should we get started?"

That was it? She was sorry and let's get started? No explanation of why she was late or . . . Aaron wasn't sure what he was looking for. More than he was getting, that was for sure. "Yeah, I guess. Traffic bad out there?"

"No more than usual for Tyson's. They started some construction by the mall—that's going to be annoying if it lasts long—but I'll just avoid route seven and come the back way for a while." Holly let out a heavy sigh as she reached into her bag for her laptop. "I spent some time last night working on the transitions between the sections so they feel more cohesive. Do you want to look on my machine? Or I can email you the file."

Aaron fought back a growl. She obviously wasn't going to take his hint. So he should let it go. Except he hated it when people were late, and he felt like she owed him an explanation. He crossed to the little table and scooted his chair close. "I'll look here."

Holly's smile was tight as she pushed the computer toward him. "Make whatever tweaks you think it needs."

He'd been planning to. He skimmed the parts he'd written, looking for anything she might have changed. Would she do that without talking to him? Surely not . . . and yet, she'd taken it on herself to work on the transitions. Whatever that meant.

He got to the end of the section. Aha. That was what she'd meant. He considered the short paragraph bridging the two sections and nodded. "That's really good."

She snorted. "Don't sound so surprised."

"I wasn't . . . " Aaron stopped and cleared his throat. "Sorry. I know you said you have a business degree, too."

"You just didn't believe me."

"No. It's not that. I just wasn't sure what to think." Geez, could she be any pricklier? "I guess you didn't wonder about my qualifications at all?"

"Not really." She sipped from her tumbler. "You're senior level. Everything I've seen or heard suggests you earned your position and do a good job. Add that to my tendency to believe people when they tell me something, and I guess I took you at your word."

Heat seared his cheeks. They were probably flaming red at this point. "Do you have kids?"

Holly stiffened and crossed her arms. "Why?"

"I don't know, you've got the mom set-down perfected. If you don't have kids, you're ready for them. Maybe they just teach that to all women."

"Oh, that? Yes, we have a special class our senior year of high school. That's also when they insert the eyes in the back of our head." Her voice held a hint of wry humor. "Should I apologize?"

"Nah. I'll tell my mom you took care of slapping me back. She'll be glad." He shrugged and returned to the document. There were a few word choices that weren't exactly what he would have used, but they weren't bad. Or wrong. Just different. In his mind, it showed enormous control that he didn't change any of them.

Well, okay, he only changed two.

Finally, he leaned back in his chair and pushed the laptop toward Holly. "I think this is ready. It's solid and even though we divvied up the work, it reads like a single, cohesive document."

Holly's grin flashed so fast, Aaron wasn't positive he saw it. "I agree. Should I go ahead and send it to Tyler?"

"Yeah. Why not?" Aaron watched as her fingers flew over the keyboard.

"What?"

"It's nothing. You're fast."

Holly laughed. "Occupational hazard, I guess."

Aaron nodded. "I can type. I don't mean to imply I can't. Still have to hunt around now and then when it comes to numbers, but it's nothing like that."

"Sure, but you're not a programmer."

Was that supposed to explain everything? It wasn't as if the majority of his work didn't happen behind the keyboard just like hers. "No."

Holly looked up. "Sent. You know that wasn't a slam, right? I just meant that programmers tend to work on their typing speed, because it means the code keeps up with our thought process."

"Uh-huh."

"I'm digging a deeper hole, aren't I? I'll stop."

He nodded, but his lips curved. "Probably wise."

She laughed.

The sparkle in her eyes caught him by surprise. She was pretty. Not that he was thinking of her that way. They were colleagues at best. And all they had to do was work together for six months until Aaron demonstrated conclusively that he was the better choice to be in charge of the social media arm of the company. Then? He wasn't going to end up having all that much to do with Holly Bell. She'd go back to being a programmer, and he'd finally get to implement the changes he kept proposing to give them an even bigger market share in the social media industry.

"Have any plans this weekend?" Aaron wasn't sure who was more surprised by the words that popped out of his mouth.

"Just church on Sunday. I try not to miss."

"Where do you go?"

Holly cocked her head to the side. "If I say the name of a church, are you going to pretend you know something about it under the misguided impression that that'll give you some kind of in with me? I don't date, if that's what you were working up to."

His mouth opened, but it took a moment for the words to work their way out. "I go to Grace—you know Pastor Brown, right? Everyone knows of Pastor Brown."

"Sure. He does little two-minute thoughts on the Christian radio station. Pastors the enormous church in Springfield."

Aaron nodded. "I've been attending there for probably four years now. I like their Saturday night service, because sleeping in is my favorite thing in the whole world and this gives me two days to do it instead of just one. Plus, it feels friendlier somehow."

Holly managed a halting nod. "I tried Grace a couple of times. It's too big for me. There's a nice, smaller church down Gallows Road a little from there, Cornerstone?"

"Sure, I've driven past it." He nodded. It definitely qualified as smaller, if the size of their parking lot was anything to go by. "How many people would you say attend there each week?"

"Maybe one fifty?" She shrugged. "I like recognizing the faces of people I sit with. Knowing names."

"I can see that. To be fair, I know most of the folks who sit near me regularly on Saturday nights at Grace, but I know what you're getting at." He smiled. It was still nice that she went to church. It didn't necessarily mean she was a believer, but it was a start.

"I guess that's the difference between introverts and extroverts."

"What do you mean?"

Holly looked down at her computer as it sounded an incoming email. "I need a smaller crowd to be comfortable getting to know the people around me. You're just as happy to have a throng and be the one reaching out. Tyler wants to see us in his office."

"You think I'm an extro . . . wait, Tyler does?"

Holly nodded.

"Does he say why?"

She shook her head and twisted the computer around so he could see the email message open on her screen.

Aaron scowled at the terse "Come see me at your earliest convenience" that made up the whole of the message. It was a reply to the email Holly had sent with the attached five-year plan. "I guess we should go. Do you want to call and see if now works, or should we just head up?"

"He said earliest convenience. I'd rather get it over with." Holly visibly swallowed. "Can I leave my things in your office?"

"Of course." Aaron stood and shoved his hands into his pockets. They hadn't done anything wrong, and yet this felt exactly like getting called into the principal's office. He'd had a lot of experience with that in high school—or the dean in college—neither was particularly pleasant.

Holly cradled her travel mug in her hands as she headed toward the elevator.

Ella smiled and waggled her eyebrows at Aaron as he walked past, following Holly. He tried to return a grin, but his face wouldn't cooperate.

The elevator was in the process of disgorging workers onto their floor. Aaron and Holly stepped on just before the doors closed.

Aaron reached over to push the button for the top floor. Three buttons between those floors were lit. People got off at each stop, but no one else got on.

When they were alone and on the way to the top floor where the executive offices were located, Holly looked over. "Do you think we're in trouble?"

"Why would we be? Because we finished like he told us to?" They'd followed the template, and the fact that they both had a business degree had, in Aaron's estimation at least, made their document solid. Reasonable.

Sure, there were a few parts that were a stretch—but they weren't outside the bounds of reality, and stretch goals were a good thing.

"I don't like this." Holly's knuckles were white as she gripped the travel mug in both hands.

"Take a breath." Aaron reached over and gently touched her arm. "Maybe he thinks it's good and wants to tell us in person."

Holly's laugh held no mirth. "Oh yeah. Because that happens."

The elevator stopped and the doors slid open. Aaron didn't reply. He just stepped off and headed toward Tyler's office.

Holly wasn't wrong. Any of the optimistic spins he tried to put on this summons seemed forced, but what else was he supposed to do?

"No, Tyler, I don't need your help. I know how to do my job. I don't remember you being like this."

Aaron's steps slowed as raised voices floated down the hall from Tyler's office. He glanced over at Holly, who was shrinking into herself even further.

"Danielle. I'm just trying to make sure you're okay. I lo—"

"Stop, would you? I don't know why you keep trying to say we have a relationship. I think I'd remember that. I just want to do my job in peace. I'd appreciate it if you wouldn't summon me to your office unless you had a valid reason." Danielle stormed out of Tyler's office, flying past them on her way to the elevators.

"Uh-oh." Aaron barely heard Holly's whisper.

"Should we try another time? I kind of assumed he was free if he was sending emails." Aaron bit his lip. What was the best choice?

"We're here. Maybe we should just get it over with."

Aaron stared at Holly for a moment before finally nodding. Delaying probably wasn't going to change whatever Tyler had to say. And yet, Aaron would rather come back at a time when the guy's ex-girlfriend hadn't just finished ripping into him. "You're sure?"

"No. But I also know I'm going to go crazy if this is hanging over my head all day."

There was that.

Aaron nodded and took a few halting steps toward Tyler's office. He reached up and knocked on the open door.

Tyler looked up, his hopeful expression rapidly shifting to one of frustration. "Come on in. Is Holly with you?"

Holly peeked around Aaron's shoulder.

"Good. That's something, at least." Tyler tented his fingers while Aaron and Holly sat in the chairs in front of his desk. "You were both in the meeting on Monday."

It wasn't a question, but Aaron found himself nodding.

"The meeting where I made it clear you needed to work together on this five-year plan."

Aaron's stomach sank. "Yes."

"So you can probably figure out what I'm going to say, right?" Tyler frowned at them.

"But we did work together." Holly's tongue darted between her lips. "You didn't expect us to sit and hover over each other's shoulders while one person typed. Right?"

"Actually, yes."

"But why?"

Aaron would have laughed at the horror in Holly's voice if this hadn't been so serious. Was he going to lose his chance at the position right out of the gate?

"Because that's what Joe wants." Tyler blew out a breath. "Look. I can tell that you did spend some time together working on it—but it's also pretty obvious that you divvied it up and melded the final product. Don't do that. When we say work together, we mean work together."

"That's a lot of extra time. I just—if the final product is right, why do you care how we got there?"

Aaron glanced over at Holly. Why did she sound panicky now? Was working with him that horrible? "We'll do better. We're sorry."

Tyler looked between the two of them and shook his head.

"You have to know something like this is going to require work outside of normal office hours. If you want it badly enough, you're going to figure it out. Seriously. Figure it out."

"We will. Thanks, Tyler." Aaron stood, recognizing dismissal. He caught Holly's gaze and jerked his head toward the door.

"But—"

Aaron scowled and started to leave. Hopefully, she'd take the hint and follow. What he absolutely didn't need happening was her stubbornness costing him the chance to be part of this. Surely, if Joe and Tyler decided that a team wasn't working, they'd only replace the weak link, right?

Because, right now, that link was Holly. And it didn't matter how much her quiet sassiness caught his attention and made him think she'd be someone fun to get to know. He had plenty of friends.

Holly needed to get on board or get out of the way.

"Come on, Mom!" Luca danced in a circle around Holly as she stared at the jars of pickles on the shelf. "I don't even like pickles."

"But I do." She glanced at him with a smile. Why couldn't she concentrate? They were pickles, for crying out loud. The fate of the world didn't hinge on what she took home. Holly grabbed a small jar of bread-and-butter pickles and added them to the cart. Then, frowning, she reached for dill spears. It was okay to buy two jars. There were no pickle police.

"Two? Blech." Luca stuck out his tongue. "I'm not eating any of them."

Holly laughed and ruffled his hair. "Noted, counselor. What's next on the list?"

"Aw, c'mon, Mom." He smoothed his hair back in place

before looking at the piece of paper. He drew a line through an item, before squinting at the next one. "Cheese."

"Onward to the dairy aisle." Holly bit her lip as Luca led the way. He was squinting at things a lot these days. His schoolwork was fine—or, at least, the teacher hadn't reached out about anything. But maybe she needed to juggle a trip to the eye doctor into the schedule somewhere. All the worries about time and expense flitted through her head, but she ignored them. If she'd gotten adept at anything in the last nine years, it was at ignoring the worries that cropped up when she couldn't do anything about them.

There were so few things she could actually do anything about.

She looked at her son, and her heart swelled.

They were okay. Maybe none of this was how she'd planned her life, but that didn't mean it wasn't exactly where she wanted to be. Not now, at least. "Your eyes okay, Luca?"

He shrugged.

That was his typical answer. How was his day? Shrug. Learn anything interesting? Shrug. So, maybe it wasn't anything to worry about. Except . . . a thirty-minute visit to the eye doctor was easy enough to arrange.

So she'd arrange it.

He'd get to leave school early and she'd get out of work and maybe they'd splurge on ice cream, because why not?

She'd call first thing Monday morning.

"What kind of cheese? There are a zillion types." Luca gestured to the case.

"There are. Do you eat all of those types?"

Luca made a face and shook his head.

"Okay, so you think maybe we should choose the kind you actually eat?"

He laughed and reached for a block of cheddar and a package of American singles. "Just checking."

"Uh-huh. Think maybe someday you'll want to branch out to something new, like maybe Monterey Jack?"

Luca shrugged.

Holly laughed. How had she known that would be his response? "All right, you. Next?"

"Chips." He turned and pointed to the chip aisle. "I can go get them and bring them back. You can get the yogurt."

She considered the distance to the chips and had to force herself to take a deep breath. It was fine. Good, even, for him to show this little bit of independence. It wasn't as if she wouldn't be able to see him nearly the whole time. "Okay. Only one bag though."

"But—"

"One. Bag." Holly held his gaze until his shoulders sank and he nodded. "Ready? Go."

With a grin and a muffled whoop, Luca darted down the row of chips. Holly watched until he scooted out of sight then turned to the yogurt, directly across from the cheese. She reached for the single brand that Luca would deign to eat and added two containers to her cart.

"Holly?"

She turned. Her stomach sank when she spotted Aaron. Why was he here on a Friday night? Shouldn't he be out partying or on a date? "Aaron. Hi."

"Looks like you know how to live it up the same as I do." He chuckled and reached for a variety pack of Greek yogurt.

"So it seems." Her gaze darted to Luca as he came back into view with an enormous bag of chips in his arms. Everything in her tensed. "I guess I'm surprised."

His eyebrows lifted. "A guy's gotta eat."

"True." Why were her hands sweating? She wiped them on

her jeans and slung an arm around Luca as he dropped the bag of chips in the cart.

"You got the yogurt, Mom?" Luca peered into the cart before drawing a line through an item on the list. "Next is eggs."

Holly offered Aaron a tight smile. "Enjoy your evening."

"You, too."

She caught a glimpse of Aaron standing still, his little hand-basket looped over his arm, staring after them. Well, let him stare. She wasn't the only single mother in the world. For all Aaron knew, she was married and just didn't wear a ring. There was a reason she kept her private life private. She fought the urge to glance back and see if he was still watching.

"What's after eggs?"

Luca sighed and squinted at the list. "Waffles. Can we get pizza?"

"Is it on the list?"

"It's never on the list."

Holly's lips twitched. "Never?"

"Fine. Hardly ever." Luca sighed and opened the egg case. He took out a dozen, flipped up the lid, and started wiggling each egg. "I still don't see why you hafta touch them."

Holly put her hand on his and moved it back to the egg he'd skipped. "Do that one again."

Luca pushed on it and frowned. "Why doesn't it wiggle?"

Holly pointed to the edges where egg had dried. "It's broken. See here? So it's stuck to the container. Which means when we got it home, if we hadn't checked, we wouldn't have all twelve eggs that we needed."

"You can use a broken egg. You have to break them to use them."

She couldn't fault his logic. "You're not wrong. But it might not be safe, because we're not the ones who did the breaking. Put that container back and try another one."

Luca did as he was told. This time, the eggs were all fine and he set it carefully in the cart. "Waffles."

"Yep. While I get a box of frozen waffles, why don't you go choose a pizza?"

"Really?" His eyes lit up with hope.

Holly smiled into his shining face. "Really. It's Friday night. We deserve to live a little."

Luca threw his arms around her and squeezed her so tight it was hard to get her breath. "You're the best mom ever!"

She'd take the win. They didn't come as easily as they had when he was younger. And he was only nine. What would it be like when he was a full-on teenager?

She had four years before she had to find out for sure, although the mom groups and blogs said that "tween" could be almost as bad. Still, nine wasn't quite a tween, either.

Holly grabbed the box of frozen waffles and went around the frozen case to find Luca staring intently at the pizza options, his tongue caught between his teeth, a sure sign of concentration.

She glanced toward the end of the aisle, trying not to let her impatience show. Pizza was a big deal, and she didn't need to rush his enjoyment of the process. No matter how much she didn't want to run into Aaron Powell.

She wouldn't be able to avoid introducing Luca if they bumped into each other again. And Holly wasn't in the mood to tell the whole story. Not to someone from work. Certainly not to someone like Aaron Powell.

He was handsome and together and had probably never made a wrong move in his life. Which meant he'd be one more judgmental person to have to ignore. And that would be a challenge when they had to work together for this contest.

She let out a little sigh. So she'd concocted some harmless little daydreams about Aaron. They didn't hurt anyone. But maybe now it was time to let them go.

Luca opened the case and grabbed a box. "This one."

"Perfect. Come on, let's finish this list and get home. You want to watch a movie while we eat?"

"Can I choose it?"

"You bet."

"Yay!"

"Tell you what. Let's grab some ice cream and make it a party." Holly smiled at the joy on her son's face and pushed all thoughts of Aaron out of her mind.

She didn't need a man in her life. She had all the love she needed right here.

3

Holly dropped Luca off at his Sunday school classroom, waved to his teacher, and then made her way down the hall to the room where her group met. The church wasn't large enough to have a small group that was only women or single moms—they probably had more than one option like that where Aaron went. She'd tried Grace, and it was a lovely church. Pastor Brown was a fantastic preacher.

But it was also enormous.

What'd they have, seven services? Something like that. Plus they streamed online. And, okay fine, sometimes she'd watch the sermon on Sunday afternoon if she had spare time. But that was because Pastor Brown was good at his job.

She liked Cornerstone. The pastor here was good, too. Though sometimes he lost her. Holly could admit that. She was smart when it came to computers, but theology? It was a bigger struggle for her to wrap her head around.

When she'd found out she was pregnant just before the end of her junior year of college, her roommate had told her it was all part of God's will. Even today, Holly didn't know how she felt about that. Luca was amazing. She wouldn't trade him for the world. Now. But at the time? It had seemed incredibly unfair that one mistake had ended up with such a long-term consequence.

"Holly! You made it." Jean, one of the older married women who was part of the small group leadership team, patted the seat beside her. "We missed you last week."

"Oh. Thanks. Luca started feeling off during the service so we went home. Didn't Darla tell you?" Holly frowned slightly. She'd taken the time to hunt down her friend to make sure Jean was told.

"She did. We still missed you."

"Oh. Well, thanks." Holly took the seat beside Jean and held her Bible on her lap. She'd rather sit just about anywhere else, but there was no point in being rude. Jean was nice. She just had this image of the lonely single mom and applied it to Holly, regardless of the facts. "How was your week?"

Jean started in to a detailed retelling of her busy past several days. Holly nodded at the pauses. The other class members—mostly couples of varying ages—came in and took seats at the table.

Landon, the only other single person who consistently attended the class, made his way toward her and sat. "Hi, Jean. Holly."

"Oh, Landon." Jean leaned around Holly to grin at the man. "I thought of you this week when I saw that the youth are planning a spring break trip to the beach. Did you see that?"

"I did. I'm already signed up to chaperone." He shifted to pin Holly with his gaze. "You should come."

"Oh. Well, the youth aren't really my thing." Holly glanced toward the door. Was it too late to fake an illness and head home?

"Aw, they're fun. You'd enjoy it. And we can always use someone to help with the girls."

"I'll think about it." She offered a tight smile. There couldn't be anything worse than trying to chaperone hormonal teenage girls at the beach. Who would volunteer for that? Plus, what was she supposed to do with Luca? It wasn't like she was going to drag her nine-year-old to the beach with the youth group. "I'm part of a big contest at work right now, though, so I'm not sure taking a week off is going to be possible."

Landon's face fell. "Oh. Well, maybe you could ask? We always need more adults. And I'd enjoy a chance to get to know you better."

Holly fought to turn her wince into a smile. He was always saying stuff like that, and she just didn't look at him that way. He was a nice man. A good one. And there was probably someone out there who would be the perfect woman for him. It just wasn't going to be her. "Landon—"

He waved it off. "I know. You've told me. I just—if you change your mind, let me know."

"Okay." Should she mention it wasn't going to happen? No. That would be unreasonably mean. "Thanks."

Jean's husband, Frank, cleared his throat and called the class to order.

Holly tried to focus on Frank's opening prayer, but Landon was uncomfortably close. Everything felt close. And hot. She took a deep breath through her nose and held it, counting quietly in her head before letting it out. There was no need to panic. This was church. She loved the people here. They loved her. She was safe here.

Landon backed off.

And okay, maybe she shouldn't have had to ask him to stop asking her out more than once, but this wasn't a perfect world, and he really hadn't been too awful.

Frank ended his prayer and flipped to the chapter of the

book they were studying. She'd forgotten hers. Again. Why couldn't they just study the Bible? She always had that with her.

She tried to follow along as best as she could. Landon shifted his book over, and she could have shared, but after spurning his advances, she really didn't want to do anything that he could misconstrue as interest.

At the end of the class, Frank tented his hands in front of himself on the table and glanced from person to person. "What can we pray for this week?"

Around the table, some mentioned their children and school woes. Life with teenagers. Job concerns.

Holly wrote them down. She'd put the list on her fridge and try to pray for them every time she was in the kitchen cooking. That was working so far.

She cleared her throat. "I'm up for a big promotion at work."

The weight of everyone looking at her made her want to shrink into herself. Why had she started talking?

"That's great. When will you find out?" Frank jotted a note on his phone.

"Not until July, probably. It's a contest, kind of, where we're paired up and we have to prove that we can handle it. Kind of." It wasn't until she started explaining that Holly realized how odd Joe's setup was.

"That's unique." Frank smiled. "I guess it's one way to make sure you really know who you're promoting."

"Something like that. Anyway. I'd really like to win. It could be so amazing for me and Luca—it's an opportunity that doesn't come up very often. Probably less than once in a lifetime."

"We'll pray for God's will." Jean reached over and patted Holly's hand.

Right. That was the better response, wasn't it? The more Christian one? Except what Holly wanted was for it to be God's will for her to win. Was that not okay? Now wasn't the time to get into it. Nor was Jean the one to dig into it with. At best, she'd defer to Frank. At worst, it would get around the church that Holly didn't understand how God's will worked.

Which, okay, she didn't. But she didn't need the entire congregation knowing that.

Did gossip fly at big churches like Grace the same way it did at the smaller ones?

Frank prayed again and dismissed the class.

Holly stood and gathered her Bible to her chest. She offered smiles to the people who greeted her and slipped through the door into the crowd of people making their way to the kids' classrooms.

"Are you working at Robinson Enterprises?" Landon fell into step beside her. "I heard they're having a contest like that."

Holly sighed. "Yeah. I guess I didn't realize the contest was public knowledge."

Landon waggled his hand from side to side. "I don't know that I'd call it public knowledge. But it's not a huge secret or anything, is it?"

"I don't know. They didn't say anything about keeping quiet, but it also didn't seem like something that would make the water cooler rounds elsewhere."

Landon laughed. "It's exactly the kind of thing people talk about. You have to know that."

"Yeah, probably." She poked her head into Luca's classroom and waved.

Luca jumped from his seat and dashed toward the door.

"Luca." The teacher smiled at Holly and pointed Luca back to his table, "Crayons away first, please."

With a groan, Luca stomped back to where he'd been sitting and grumpily scooped crayons back into a tub. He grabbed a piece of paper and the tub and shuffled to the cubbies that ran along the wall. He shoved the crayons into an empty spot and frowned at the teacher. "Now?"

"Now. Have a good week."

"Was he okay?" Holly put a hand on Luca's shoulder when he stopped in front of her.

"Oh, he was fine. You know how boys get sometimes." The teacher shook her head. "See you next week, Luca."

"I guess. Bye." Luca tipped his face up to meet Holly's gaze. "Can we go now?"

"Yeah, let's get you home. Maybe it's a napping afternoon."

"Aw, Mom."

"Shh." Holly turned and started toward the exit, Luca at her side.

"Can I take you two to lunch?"

Holly glanced over at Landon. "Thanks for the offer, but no."

He slowed and held up his hands. "All right. Have a nice week."

Guilt swamped her, but she steeled herself against it. If she gave in—or even said something like "maybe another time"—Landon would take it as encouragement. She didn't want to encourage him. "Thanks. You, too."

Luca pushed open the door to the parking lot. "Come on, Mom."

She hurried her pace, ruffling Luca's hair as she reached him. "You need to stop giving your Sunday school teacher a hard time."

"She kept going on about everyone's dad. Then she got to me and made a big deal about how I don't have one." Luca crossed his arms. "I don't like her."

"Oh, baby." Holly's heart broke. "I'll talk to her."

"No. Mom, just leave it alone. But maybe I could skip Sunday school next week?"

Given how much she wanted a break from her own class,

that seemed like a good idea. "Maybe we'll go visit a different church entirely next week. Would that be fun?"

"Maybe. I'm hungry."

Holly chuckled and unlocked the car. "Then I guess it's a good thing we're on the way home."

Luca climbed in and reached for his seatbelt. "Can I have the leftover pizza from Friday?"

"Sure." She didn't want it, though she'd been planning to take it for lunch on Monday. That was more because she hadn't figured it would get eaten otherwise.

The pizza brought Aaron to mind. Did he really shop there? Why hadn't she run into him before? It all seemed so unlikely. There were literally hundreds of grocery options in the area. She tended to spread her business around between three stores, depending on when she worked shopping into her schedule.

Maybe he did, too, and that was why they normally missed each other.

Holly pointed the car toward the townhouse she'd managed to buy eighteen months ago. It was nice to be out of the apartment they'd been renting before that. Luca didn't care about equity, or anything like that, but he appreciated having more space for his things. And the backyard. He spent a lot of time out in their small fenced area.

If she got this promotion, they'd be able to afford a house. One with more than a postage-stamp-sized play area.

She'd keep her eye on the prize and not on the hotness of Aaron Powell.

∼

"I'M glad I bumped into you, man." Aaron pointed across the crowded sub shop to an empty booth. "Let's snag that."

Ian Hayes grinned and shouldered through the clump of

people waiting at the pickup end of the counter. He shrugged out of his coat and dumped it on one of the hard, yellow benches. "Think that'll hold it?"

"It should." Aaron dropped his own coat on the other side and eyed the line. "These look mostly like dads who are getting take-home orders anyway."

"Kinda do, don't they?" Ian made his way to the line of people waiting to order. "Don't you usually do the Saturday night service?"

"Yeah." Aaron scanned the menu board above the sandwich prep line. He'd probably end up with an Italian combo—it was his usual—but it never hurt to check.

"And you changed because?"

"I don't know." He'd had a hard time settling on Friday night after grocery shopping. "I didn't sleep well on Friday and then I napped—and I probably could have rushed and made it without an issue, but I wasn't feeling it."

"Hmm." Ian's gaze cut over to Aaron as they shuffled closer to their turn to order. "You get called into Tyler's office on Friday?"

"Yeah, but that's not why I couldn't sleep. That's just bogus. Dividing up the work is smart, and I think making a big deal out of doing things the smart way is stupid."

Ian laughed. "Tell me how you really feel."

"Tell me you don't agree."

"Eh. They were pretty clear they're looking for us to work together. They said that right there in the meeting. Trotted out synergy and everything."

Aaron frowned. Sure, fine. Ian was right. And Tyler had driven the point home on Friday, but it was still dumb. "I guess. So we'll spend the rest of the contest working harder, not smarter."

Ian grinned and stepped up to the counter. He ordered his

sandwich and slid down toward the next section of the assembly line where he started to point to vegetables as he asked for them.

Aaron stepped forward. "I'll do a foot-long Italian on the herb and cheese bread."

So much for branching out. But why mess with something he knew he liked? It was all part of that working smarter thing—just in this case, it was lunching smarter. Or something like that. He went through the topping process, grabbed a little bag of chips from the basket hanging on the front of the case, and snagged a cup for the soda fountain before paying.

Ian had already filled his drink and was sitting with his hands folded on top of his sandwich when Aaron made it over to their booth.

"You want me to pray?"

Aaron looked up from wrestling with the straw wrapper. "Sure."

"Thank You, Jesus, for this food and for the good conversation I know we'll have over lunch. Give Aaron and me both wisdom for this contest—let us be in Your will and not blinded by greed. Amen."

"Amen." Blinded by greed. Was he? Aaron didn't think so, but would he recognize it if it was a problem? "You're really worried about the greed thing?"

"I dunno. A little, I guess. I mean, come on, we're worth what, seven hundred mil over in games? Being in charge of something like that is going to come with perks. Big ones. And a lot of temptation." Ian unwrapped his sub and pulled half of it away so he could take a bite. "Melanie—she's who I'm paired up with—is all about the in-game story line. I think she's there because she loves what she does, and she's good at it. She'd probably keep doing it if they stopped paying her. But me? I'm a marketing guy. I already have to fight off greed on a daily basis."

Huh. Aaron hadn't thought about that. "Do you regret saying yes?"

"Nah. This is an incredible opportunity. I figure God'll protect me since I'm keeping my eyes open, you know?"

Aaron offered a thoughtful nod as he bit into his sub.

"So, if it wasn't the contest that kept you up on Friday, what was it?"

"I ran into Holly at the grocery store."

"Holly?"

"Holly Bell. She's my teammate-slash-competition."

"Ah. Right. Sorry, I don't know her. Pretty sure I might be able to pick her out of a lineup now, but that's only because of the meeting on Monday." Ian grinned and opened his chip bag. "So, what, you're astonished that grown women need groceries too?"

"She has a kid."

"Okay?"

Aaron opened his chips and dumped them on his sandwich wrapper. Ian was right—lots of people had kids. Even after their church conversation, it wasn't like it was impossible for her to have a kid. Obviously. Since she had one. "I guess I was just surprised."

"No, come on. Not buying it. How many people in Social you figure have kids?"

"Probably a lot of them."

Ian pointed. "Exactly. So is she married?"

Aaron shook his head. Although he didn't actually know that for certain. "She doesn't wear a ring."

"Single mom. Not unheard of. I don't understand your problem."

"I don't really, either. But she's gotta be right around my age, maybe a year or two younger. Max. And the kid was big. She had him young."

"It happens, man." Ian reached across and stole one of Aaron's chips.

"Hey." Aaron snatched Ian's bag and shook his head. Empty. Figured. He balled up the bag and tossed it at his friend.

Ian nabbed it out of the air and set it aside, chuckling. "So, your partner's a single mom. She's still hot. And *single*. You like kids. What's the problem?"

"It's not like that. At all. We barely know each other—we've had maybe six meetings together prior to this. And 'hot' isn't an issue. You know that."

"Uh-huh. Keep denying. That's gonna make me believe you. Promise." Ian shook his head and picked up the second half of his sandwich.

Wait, what? He didn't think Holly was attractive, did he? She wasn't a troll or anything. Okay, fine, she was good looking. Everyone could be, under the right circumstances. He wasn't looking at her like that. Was he? "Huh."

"You just figure out you've got a little thing for Holly?"

"I don't think we can even qualify it as a thing. It's marginal interest. At best. And now that I know she's a mom, that'll go away and we'll work together and I'll win and she'll go on being a great programmer and an asset to the company."

Ian laughed. "You've got it all figured out, don't you?"

"Like you don't?"

"Maybe. Although I pretty much figure Melanie's going to win and I'll wheedle my way into being her second in command. Tyler seemed to hint that the runner-up was going to be on tap for that."

Hmm. So Aaron would win and Holly would be his second? That . . . could be problematic. She wasn't going to be any good at being in charge *or* runner-up when she had the time constraints that a kid brought to the table. "Oh. That explains it."

Ian's eyebrows lifted.

"She was pretty adamant about her work hours and when she could and couldn't meet up—once we realized we had to sit together to do all the work. It's the kid."

"Bingo. Why wouldn't she just say that?"

"Not sure. I'm trying to picture her cube and I don't think she has any photos of him out, either. Or anything personal, for that matter. It's just a workspace—like she'd be ready to move out in a heartbeat."

"Weird."

"Very." Aaron wiped his fingers on a napkin and got out his phone. He tapped on the icon for Social and hit the magnifying glass as soon as it loaded. He put in Holly's name and selected the profile that had her picture on it. They weren't connected—he went ahead and sent that request while he was in there—and her profile was pretty barren. He swiveled the phone around. "Look at this. She's not really on here, either. Isn't that weird for someone who works at the company?"

Ian pulled Aaron's phone closer and scrolled up a little. "Maybe she has the security locked down and you won't see anything until you're connected."

"Possible, I guess. It's just strange." Aaron took his phone back and put it away. "It's almost like she's hiding him."

"It's okay to be a private person."

"Yeah." It was. At some level, Aaron got that—even admired it. But what he couldn't quite bring himself to say out loud to Ian was that Holly's little boy reminded him of himself. A lot. To the degree that he'd had to stop himself from digging through his old scrapbooks or calling his mom to ask her to send him photos of himself when he was in elementary school.

If he and Holly were the same age and the kid was nine or ten? Well, he hadn't been living for Jesus a decade ago. From his junior year of high school through college, he'd been steeped in rebellion against all the things his conservative Christian parents had wanted him to believe in.

Had he fathered a child somewhere along the line?

It seemed possible—but surely any woman he'd slept with would have tracked him down. He wouldn't have shirked his responsibilities—oh, he probably wouldn't have volunteered for diaper duty and night feedings, but he would have stepped up when it came to child support.

Holly's child couldn't be his.

He didn't remember her. There was nothing to suggest they'd ever crossed paths.

But what were the chances that child looked like Aaron if they didn't share DNA?

He had to find out, one way or the other.

God? I could use a little help here.

4

Aaron glanced over the five-year plan that was due to Tyler on Friday. He and Holly had found a few minutes here and there to work on it, but it wasn't finished. Not the way it could be if they'd been able to divide up the work.

As annoyed as he was, the more he thought about Holly's son, the more he wanted to keep her close and see what information he could drag out of her. Was he being paranoid?

Holly tapped on the door. She always seemed to be hanging back—like she was trying to avoid notice. Was she? "Hi. Am I early?"

"Right on time." Aaron smiled and gestured to the chair he'd dragged around to the working side of his desk. "Have a seat. I figured it'd be easier to work here, where we have two big monitors, rather than trying to hunch around a laptop screen."

"Oh. Sure." Holly set her laptop on his round table and skirted the desk. "I think we're almost done?"

"Yeah. This section," Aaron scrolled until the heading he'd been looking at was at the top of the monitor, "needs some more work. What we have is pretty standard."

"Is there something wrong with standard?"

"Probably not. Except it doesn't stand out, you know? We want our stuff to shine and make an impact. The basic boiler-plate anyone can find online is unlikely to do that."

"Right." She leaned forward and the cross on the end of the delicate gold chain around her neck slipped out from under her collar. It glinted in the light as it dangled and drew Aaron's eye to her neck.

Had he kissed her there, when they were younger and he'd been drunk? Would she have been drunk, too? If she'd been sober, wouldn't she recognize him? Remember him? If she did, wouldn't she say something?

How was he supposed to bring it up? It didn't seem like something he could just say. *So, I was wondering if you remember hooking up with me ten years ago.* Yeah. No.

"Okay, what about this?" Holly reached for the keyboard and dragged it closer. Her fingers flew across the keys.

Aaron read the words as she put them in and nodded. "That's a lot better. Do I remember you saying you have a business degree?"

A little furrow appeared between her eyebrows as she continued typing. "Maybe? I double-majored."

"Where?"

Holly stopped typing and cocked her head to the side. "Virginia Tech. Why?"

"Just curious." He hadn't gone to Tech. He'd been at James Madison. But he'd had friends at Tech and had driven down for parties on many a weekend. It was possible—very possible—that he could have run into her at one of those blowouts. He had a lot of college weekends that were only dim, blurry memories.

"What about you? Were you at Tech? It's such a huge campus, I feel like I could have gone to school with everyone I meet and, unless we were in the same major, the chance of knowing them is practically nonexistent."

He chuckled and prayed it didn't sound as frantic as it felt. "Nah. JMU."

"That's a good school, too. Did you like it?"

"I did. Although I guess it's safest to say I'm not proud of the person I was in college."

Holly nodded. She scrolled the document and pointed to the monitor when she stopped. "Should we add to this section as well? It's another that's fairly standard."

So much for that conversation. He'd opened the door, and she'd shut it firmly in his face. Fine. He'd let it rest for now. But he was going to keep trying to find ways to open it back up. If she asked what he was up to, well, how else was he supposed to get to know her? Aaron read the paragraph and frowned. "It might be standard, but what else are we supposed to say? Growth is an important part of any five-year plan. If we don't talk about it, we're setting ourselves up to get laughed at. At best."

"True." Holly drummed her fingers on the keyboard. "Maybe we can find a more creative way to say basically the same thing we have here?"

"Ugh. I guess, but I hate that. What's the point in doing all kinds of mental manipulation to sound fancy when these words get the point across and, bonus, don't sound like we're trying to sound smarter than we are?"

Holly laughed. "Let's leave it, then. Tyler didn't say anything about it in his review, right?"

"Not that I recall. Turn the markup back on and we can double-check."

"You turned the markup off?" Holly sat back, confusion written in her features. "I didn't even know you could do that."

"Sure." Aaron reached for the mouse, his hand brushing

against hers before she pulled it away. He ignored the little zing of awareness and clicked the document settings. Green bubbles appeared in the sidebar with Tyler's initials at the top. "Looks like he noted it was standard but also acknowledged there weren't really better words to use."

"So we can leave it."

"That would be my take."

Holly nodded. "Okay. Um."

"What?"

"Are you going to leave the markup in?"

"I can hide it again if you want."

"No, I just—don't you delete it as you address it?" Her hand made a little jerky movement toward the mouse.

Aaron moved his hand out of the way, a grin tugging at his lips. "I never have. I've always just hidden it. But we can do it your way."

Holly grabbed the mouse and clicked on the comment bubble, then chose "delete" from the popup menu.

"Better?"

She laughed. "Much. It really doesn't bother you?"

He shrugged. Was it supposed to? "Nope."

Holly studied him.

Aaron's heart sped. But that was ridiculous. He wasn't attracted to Holly. She wasn't attracted to him. They were coworkers and nothing more.

Unless, of course, they shared a son.

Big "if." One he currently had no idea how to discover the truth of, for that matter.

She cleared her throat. "Could we go back to the top and work through the comments?"

"Deleting as we go?" He smirked. "Sure. Why not? I don't have anywhere to be tonight. Is your husband taking care of your son?"

Holly stiffened and focused on the monitor. "No husband. I have a friend watching him, because I wasn't sure how late we'd need to work."

Well, that was something, at least. He smiled. "He's cute. I don't know a lot about kids—how old is he?"

"Nine."

Aaron waited, but no more information was forthcoming.

"I don't agree with this comment." Holly highlighted the bubble on the screen. "I can see where he's coming from, but it doesn't apply when you take into consideration that we do social media. We have to be agile enough to change with the trends—or, better, shape the trends. We can't say we're only going to apply tried and tested solutions to our business model."

Aaron leaned closer and re-read the comment. He snorted. "Yeah, that's crazy. Maybe what we need to do is address that—the why of it—here. We need to be innovators in the social media sphere. Honestly, it'd be good to do more to get out in front of the competition. We're always lagging about a half-step behind the big guys."

"More like two and a half." Holly muttered as she deleted the comment bubble and arrowed through the lines on the screen. "Here. We could add something in this section."

"Yeah, that's a good spot. Do you really think we're that far behind?" As far as Aaron could tell, their demographics were in the right range for social media users. Maybe even trending on the younger edges.

Holly waggled her hand from side to side before returning to typing. "I guess it's more that we don't innovate. Ever. We just follow in the footsteps of what we see someone else doing. And it's not that there aren't ideas. I sit in the development meetings where good idea after good idea is tossed around, written up, submitted, and then it's crickets for weeks. By the time we get an okay to even start researching something, two other platforms have announced a release date for the same thing—or something close enough that it might as well be the same."

"You think we have someone leaking ideas?"

"Nah. When you're immersed in this world, the ideas are there, you know. It's a matter of nailing them down." She frowned, added another sentence, then leaned back. "What do you think of this?"

Aaron scrolled up to the top of the section and read. He smiled. "This is good. Really good."

Pink washed over Holly's cheeks. "Thanks."

"We should add something about seizing innovation opportunities more rapidly. Maybe here?" Aaron placed the cursor where it seemed like it would be easy to add a word or two.

"Sure." Holly adjusted the text and glanced over her shoulder at him. "Ready to go on?"

His breath caught, and he started to drift, just for a moment, into her eyes.

No no no. He was *not* attracted to Holly. He barely knew her.

He nodded. "Yep. Let's move on. What time do you have to be home for—what was your son's name again?"

Holly sighed. "His name's Luca, and my friend is happy to hang out at our place as long as I need her to. She likes the quiet after he goes to bed and is willing to help with fractions as a tradeoff. That said, if we're not going to be finished by six, six thirty, I'd like to order in food. I get grumpy when my blood sugar starts dropping."

Aaron grinned at the influx of information. Her friend was another woman, not the guy she was seeing. Her son's name was Luca. And it wouldn't take much to stretch this into a dinner meeting. And dinner meetings were basically the same thing as dates.

～

HOLLY LEANED on the grocery cart and trudged behind it as Luca rattled off the items on their list. Friday night grocery shopping. How much more fun could anyone ask for?

"Mom, did you hear me?"

"No, sorry, honey. I was thinking. What did you ask?"

"I know you don't want pizza, but what if we got taquitos? They're easy. I could probably even make them myself—I know how to put things in the oven and get them out. Then we could watch *Hulk* and eat on the couch."

Holly fought a wince. *Hulk* was not on the list of movies she was excited to watch—it always meant two or three days of Luca stomping around yelling "SMASH!" while flexing. It was cute the first six thousand times he did it.

Maybe it would still be cute if she wasn't so darn tired.

"So? Can we?"

She looked at the hopeful, toothy grin on her son's face and had to smile. "Why not? It's Friday."

"Grocery shopping on Friday is the best!" Luca raced down the aisle and yanked open one of the freezer case doors. "Chicken or beef?"

"Chicken is better." A familiar male voice answered from behind her.

Holly stiffened and turned to look over her shoulder. "Are you following me?"

Aaron snorted. "Nope. Turns out, I have this new project at work that means I end up having less time to grocery shop. But unless I was going to eat Lucky Charms for dinner, I needed to stop here on my way home."

"Lucky Charms? What grown man eats Lucky Charms?" She shook her head, not sure if she should buy his explanation or not.

"Oh, come on. They're magically delicious." Aaron winked at

Luca, who laughed like a loon. "I'm serious about the taquitos though—get the chicken. The beef are weird."

"Here." Luca dropped the box in the cart and looked between Holly and Aaron. "Do you know my mom?"

Holly blinked and deflated. She didn't like introducing Luca to people—he glommed on to them so easily and then was heartbroken when they faded out of his life. "This is Mr. Powell, honey. He works with me. Aaron, my son, Luca."

"Nice to meet you, Luca." Aaron held out his hand.

Luca studied it a moment before giving it a firm shake. "You, too."

Holly watched Aaron's face and could see him holding back words. "What?"

Aaron shook his head. "I'll ask you on Monday."

She frowned.

"Can we get soda, too?"

Holly zeroed in on her son's face, eyebrows raised. "What do you think?"

Luca sighed. "No. Juice?"

Holly squeezed her eyes shut as a dull throb started in her temples. "What if we made fizzy water at home? I'll add a little lemon and sugar."

"Yes!" Luca pumped his fist and looked at Aaron. "Mom makes the best fizzy lemonade. Have you had it? You should come over—we're watching *Hulk* while we eat. Have you seen it?"

"No, I haven't."

"Really? I thought grownups got to watch movies whenever they wanted and not just on Fridays, when they stayed on green at school the *whole* week and did all their chores, too."

Aaron chuckled. "I actually have to do all my chores before I can watch movies, too. That never goes away."

Huh. Who would have thought Aaron would be good with

kids? She'd been braced for him to say something that would undermine her attempts to teach Luca responsibility. Why? It seemed like everyone did.

"Oh. Well, you should come. Can he, Mom?" Luca turned to look at Holly, his eyes wide, "He's never seen *Hulk*."

"That is sad, but I'm sure Mr. Powell has a lot he needs to do tonight." Holly ruffled Luca's hair. "It was nice of you to think of him, though."

"I don't, actually." Aaron's eyebrows lifted and mischief glinted in his eyes. "Taquitos, fizzy lemonade, and *Hulk* is a pretty amazing offer."

"Oh. But. I. We. You." She stopped and swallowed. Her heart hammered in her chest. Why would he do that? Why wouldn't he just excuse himself like a normal person? Who took a kid up on an invitation? Her mind was racing. She tried to stay on top of the housekeeping, but there were days when she got home and all she had the energy for was homework, bath time, reading, and bed. Half the time, she ended up heading to bed within thirty minutes of tucking Luca in. "I'm not sure there'll be enough."

"We can get another box. They're only three dollars." Luca reached for the freezer door again.

Holly breathed in deeply. "No, it's okay. I'll make a salad to go with them. You don't have perishable items that need to get put away?"

"I'm assuming you live close. I do, too. So maybe I can drop them off on my way." Aaron grinned. He leaned close and his breath tickled her ear as he whispered, "I didn't mean to put you on the spot. I can make an excuse if it's a problem."

Drat the man. Now he was being nice about it? The fact was, he *had* put her on the spot. But Luca seemed so excited. "It's okay. We're over off Heritage in the new construction."

"Sure. I know that area. I can definitely drop mine off and meet you there. Can I bring something for dessert?"

Excitement shone from Luca's face, but he knew better than to ask for sweets.

Holly forced her lips to curve. "Sure. That would be great. I guess we'll see you soon."

"Here. If you want to put your number in, and maybe add your actual address? Otherwise, I can call you when I get close." Aaron offered his phone.

Right. She took it and added the information he'd need. It was good for him to have it. They had the contest to think about. He wasn't likely to use it for anything other than work stuff, anyway.

They'd shared a meal on Wednesday because they'd been working late. Now, he was coming over because Luca hadn't appropriately internalized the concept of stranger danger—or whatever it was they were calling it now. Tricky people? Aaron definitely qualified there, that was for sure. Except he wasn't bad. Just mischievous.

It was better to focus on that than the little quiver of antici-pation that sparked in her belly. She wasn't interested in Aaron Powell. It had just been a long time since a man—well, other than Landon—had given her the time of day.

There was no harm in enjoying the attention.

She wasn't going to do anything about it.

5

Holly set the folder containing details about the February challenge for the contest aside and wiggled her mouse. When the monitor turned on, she typed in her password and switched to her email program. Why did it feel like she got further behind the more she accomplished? Was that what winning would be like? Would it be go-go-go all the time with no break? And if it was, did she want that?

Maybe she should bow out.

It would solve the problem of spending all that time with Aaron, if nothing else.

She hadn't bumped into him outside of work since he weaseled his way into a dinner invitation two weeks ago, but that was primarily because she'd changed grocery stores. There were options—it was one of the benefits of living in the Metro DC area—there were always options for anything you needed. But the reality was, she missed her usual store. The cost was about the same, but the brands were just different enough that Luca made yucky faces about things. And that got old. Quickly.

Maybe this week they'd switch and do the groceries on Thursday.

Or she could grow up and just talk to Aaron and ask him to leave her alone.

Holly shook her head and clicked on another email, scanning the contents before deleting it. Not her problem to deal with, but some of the programmers liked to include everyone in their conversations. Why? Who knew.

The next was the overnight server traffic report. This was the second night in a row there had been unusual spikes around two a.m. Nothing huge—probably not a red flag—but she'd keep an eye on it.

"Hey."

Holly jolted and spun in her chair. "Aaron. Hi. What's up?"

"You took off after the meeting kind of fast. You okay?"

"Sure. Yes. Of course. It's Monday—busy day, you know?" *Take the hint and move along.* He had to have more to do himself, didn't he?

"Right." Aaron tucked his hands in the pockets of his slacks and leaned against the opening of her cube. "The thing is, I've noticed you haven't been grocery shopping on Fridays. And that you're very—hmm, let's call it efficient—with your time when we have a scheduled meeting. So I wondered if I'd done something that made you uncomfortable or upset."

Holly swallowed. Direct confrontation was not her forte. Hadn't she changed grocery stores to avoid precisely this situation? She bit her lip. "Do you have a couple of minutes to go get a coffee?"

His eyebrows lifted. "Okay."

She turned back to her machine and locked it before grabbing her purse out of the bottom file drawer and standing. She reached for her coat, but he beat her to it and held it open. Her cheeks heated, but she smiled and slipped her arms into the sleeves. "Do you need to get anything from your office?"

"Not unless we're walking farther than the coffee shop on the corner."

"That's fine." They made a good mocha. And okay, it wasn't her treat day, but she'd just move things around in the budget— being a single mom meant she'd learned to be flexible when necessary.

Aaron grinned.

They walked in silence to the elevators. Holly could practically feel the eyes of her coworkers as they passed cubes. She was probably imagining it. But several of the people who sat around her thrived on gossip. It was why she wanted to talk outside the office in the first place. The ride down to the ground floor and the walk through the chilly, February wind were quiet as well.

Holly considered and discarded several banal conversational topics. She didn't need to fill the silence just because she could. And if he needed it filled, he could say something.

Except, of course, that the lack of conversation made it so she couldn't avoid noticing him. He was so *male*. Not in an over-the-top jock way, but everything about him had her nerve endings on alert. In all the right ways.

She didn't need that. Her life was Luca and work. It was a good life. It was all she had time for. And the fact that Aaron had made a deeply positive impression on Luca when he'd come for dinner was something she still didn't know how to handle.

Aaron pulled open the coffee shop door and waved her in. "Order what you like, this is my treat."

"No, that's okay. I can—"

He made an impatient noise. "Would you please let me do something nice?"

"Fine. Thank you." Holly walked stiffly to the counter and ordered a mocha. She glanced around the shop and slid to the pickup area. Her eyebrows shot up as she saw—oh what were their names? Stephanie and someone. The government services team. Holding hands. And smiling at each other the way couples did.

"Well, well, well. That's an interesting development." Aaron's voice was quiet and he nudged her side. "Don't stare or they're going to look over and see. I wouldn't have pegged that in a million years, would you?"

"I don't know them well enough to say. Maybe they're a perfect and obvious couple."

Aaron snorted. "Bzzt. Christopher's in my Bible study on Monday nights. From how he talks about her, he hates her. Or he did."

"Men never really outgrow kindergarten, do they?" Holly accepted her mocha and glanced around the tables. "Let's take the booth over by the fireplace. It's away from them and will give them some privacy."

Aaron gaped at her.

She shrugged and walked off with her drink. It hadn't escaped her notice that all the teams in the contest were a man and a woman. Hopefully, Joe and Tyler were just trying to have equal representation among the genders. The other alternative —that they were matchmaking—wasn't worth thinking about.

Before long, Aaron slid onto the seat across from her, cradling a tall cup in his hands. "Explain the kindergarten comment."

Holly sighed. "When a boy likes you in elementary school, they're mean. They pull your hair and make fun of you. And apparently that doesn't change when they get older."

Aaron's lips curved. "Have I pulled your hair or called you names?"

She blinked and leaned back in her seat. Blood roared in her ears. "No. But you don't think of me that way. We're teammates. That's it."

"Is it? Is that all we can be?"

"Aaron." Holly sipped her coffee and tried to collect her scattered thoughts. "Is that why you've been showing up at the grocery store?"

"Well, that and I need eggs and a loaf of bread. That's where they sell those things."

She lost her fight against the smile that tugged at her lips. "You asked if you'd upset me. And the answer is not really. But this thing between you and me can't happen."

"Why not? You're seeing someone already?"

"No."

"You don't find me attractive."

Heat flooded her face. "I don't know how to answer that."

"It's a yes or no question. I'm a big boy, I can take it." Aaron's eyes glinted with humor.

"It's not a matter of attraction. It's not that easy. I have a son."

"He's great. And he does a fantastic Hulk impression."

Holly looked away. Two weeks later and Luca was full of Hulk and Mr. Powell. Still. "Yes, thank you. He's my world."

"It shows." Aaron touched her hand. "I understand you're a package deal. And there are probably complications with your ex and custody. None of that scares me."

"No. Luca's father isn't in the picture."

"He's deceased? I'm sorry. That's hard."

"No." Holly blew out a breath as irritation stirred in her gut. "Look. I did something stupid in college—like people do—and it derailed things for a while. Then when I found out I was pregnant, the boy I thought was the father did all the right things. We were going to make it work. And then they had to do an amnio because they were worried about Luca's development, so he had them check paternity, just to be sure. Except it turned out he wasn't the father, after all. So then he was gone, and I was left with a souvenir from the biggest stupid thing I did in college, but I can't regret it, because Luca is my world. But it means that he has no father in his life, because I never knew the name of who that father would be. And we're doing okay. We're making it work. And I'm not going to jeopardize that just because I find you attractive and interesting and exactly the kind of man I'd want in my life if I were free to have one."

Holly scooted out of the seat and jerkily pulled on her coat. "Thank you for the coffee. I have to go."

"Holly."

She shook her head, not trusting her voice. She hadn't meant to dump all of that on him. Hardly anyone knew the full story. Her parents did. A handful of friends in college—all of whom she'd lost touch with. But people who knew her today? No way. It was better to be Holly the single mom without having to explain that her one experiment with alcohol in college had left her pregnant with only enough of a memory of the experience to know she'd been a willing participant.

Holly strode from the coffee shop without looking back. She kept her focus on the ground in front of her. She didn't spend a lot of time wishing for things to be different. There was no point. Things were what they were. And Luca? He was her heart. Her everything. That wasn't a lie.

She wouldn't wish him away.

Maybe she didn't understand the role God's will played in all of this—whether it was God's will that she get drunk and sleep with a random guy and then go off the deep end when she'd realized what she'd done and finally give in to the guy she'd been sort of dating. It didn't seem like that was something God would have willed—not when it was all sin. And yet, Luca was a blessing, not a curse.

And okay, maybe she hadn't always seen it that way, but it hadn't taken long to get there.

So maybe it was a matter of God using her messed-up life to

bring Him glory—and to bring her closer to Him. Because wasn't that at the heart of God's will?

She shook her head as her fast, long strides carried her back to the main office doors. It didn't matter. She trusted God. She loved Luca. And she'd worked hard to reach a place where she was content with the way things were in her life.

She wasn't going to let Aaron Powell disrupt that.

No matter how much he made her yearn for things she'd never known she wanted.

~

AARON WATCHED HOLLY LEAVE.

She'd left her coffee on the table.

He almost called out—but what? Like she was going to come back for it and say thank you?

His thoughts reeled.

He'd convinced himself there were hundreds of options for Luca's parentage that didn't involve him. After all, it wasn't as if he had such a unique visage that it was impossible for another child in the world to look like him with no familial relationship.

Doppelgangers were a thing.

Now, though?

Holly's story had put hot, lead weights in his belly. A party where an abundance of alcohol and easy sex were the evening's entertainment? Those had been his specialty. And he'd done plenty of driving to Tech to attend those sorts of parties when the pickings at JMU were slim.

He pressed his fingers to his eyes.

It still didn't necessarily mean anything. There were other guys who looked enough like Aaron that Luca's dad could be someone else.

But now? He had to know.

If Luca was his—and there was something deep in his soul that was filled with certainty, even though he couldn't prove or explain it—he wanted to do right by the boy. And his mother.

But how?

Aaron buried his face in his hands and cried out to God for wisdom.

He didn't know how long he'd been sitting there when his phone's vibration jolted him back to reality.

He pulled the phone free and checked the alarm. Great. If he didn't rush, he was going to be late for the monthly managers meeting. That was never a good look. Especially when Aaron knew several of the other customer experience managers were annoyed that he'd been selected for the contest and they hadn't.

Aaron drained his coffee as he hurried through the coffee shop—didn't matter that it had gone cold—and dumped the cup in the trash can as he pushed through the doors. He broke into a jog once he hit the sidewalk.

The meeting was full of subtle jabs and side-eyed looks. Aaron feigned ignorance and focused on the task at hand. It wasn't his fault he'd been chosen. He hadn't had any say in the matter. At all. Or not much. He could have turned it down. But what sort of idiot would he have to be to do that? Their jealousy would either burn out or eat them alive. Neither one was something he could control, nor was it anything he needed to worry about.

When the meeting finally ended, Aaron escaped to his office and shut the door. He was tempted to punch the little lock button beside the knob, but that was probably overkill. He was fairly certain no one was supposed to actually *use* the locks. A closed door had always been enough to keep people out before.

Aaron sat in his desk chair, leaned back, and closed his eyes. He was ready to head home. Maybe skip out on Bible study tonight and just pretend he lived alone on a deserted planet.

Mars was always good for that—although now that there was a new lander prowling around up there, maybe he needed to venture farther. Pluto? So what if it was technically a dwarf planet? It was definitely far enough away that nothing could bother him.

Except.

He sighed. Responsibilities mattered. And there were plenty of examples that proved that running away from problems never really provided the desired solution. Look at Jonah.

So he'd focus on the task and try to leave the rest of it in God's capable hands. He'd never let Aaron down yet. Even if the reverse was decidedly untrue.

His thoughts started to circle back to his college days, and it took everything he had to slam down his mental defenses. He wasn't going fishing to dredge up past sin and look it over. That was not what Jesus wanted.

Why was it so hard?

Holly. And Luca. Those were the reasons today, at least.

Aaron pushed away from his desk and headed out into cube land. He wound through the maze, absentmindedly nodding when someone greeted him. Finally, he reached Holly's cube. He stood to the side, watching her for a moment while she was unaware of his presence. She was focused—her head bowed slightly as her fingers raced across the keyboard.

Aaron glanced at her monitor then shook his head. Reading code had never been something he even desired to learn.

He cleared his throat.

Holly typed a few more words, clicked her mouse, then turned. Her polite smile faded as her gaze locked on him.

He ignored the pang in his chest and worked to keep his voice low. "Are you okay?"

"Yes."

He waited, but she didn't elaborate. Okay. Probably not the

time or place to get into it much more. Still. "We never did firm up ideas for the love-your-job task."

Her eyes rolled upward and she sighed. "I figured we could both think up ideas and discuss them Wednesday afternoon at our regularly scheduled meeting."

Right. He nodded. "Okay."

"You could have emailed me."

He waited until she met his gaze. "I know."

Her cheeks flamed pink, and she looked away. "Is that all? There's a problem with the integration of the features we've had in a limited beta for the last month. We were hoping to roll them out in phases to everyone in March, but this is a big snag."

In other words, she had work to do, and he was in her way. Aaron nodded. "I'll let you get back to it."

Why had he sought her out? He mulled it over as he made his way back to his office. He had wanted to ask about the next contest project, but Holly was right. That could have been an email.

He'd needed to see her. Make sure she really was all right. He'd known she'd say she was fine. But he hadn't known how to believe her without seeing it.

Why did he care so much?

Because he was interested in Holly. And attracted. And he was both of those things before he knew about Luca. Now? The kid was an added bonus. He was smart and interesting and full of joy. Something about having them in his life felt right.

Now all he had to do was convince Holly.

What could possibly go wrong?

6

Aaron had been watching the clock for the last half hour. Five minutes ago, he'd finally given up and closed the document he'd been working on—or pretending to—and opened up the list of ideas he'd brainstormed instead of sleeping last night.

Holly was due for their meeting in two minutes.

His muscles tensed in anticipation. He'd tried running track in high school, and this reminded him of the moments just before the starting gun, when he stood on his mark, braced and waiting.

The knock on his office door was like a blast through his senses.

"Come in."

"Hi." Holly poked her head in first, then the rest of her followed. "Are you ready?"

"Yep. Do you want to come around here again?" He gestured to the chair he'd already brought to his side of the desk. "It's easier, isn't it?"

"Sure." Her smile was cool. Distant, but not impolite. "Do you want me to type?"

He chuckled and stood, shifting around so she could squeeze past and sit in his desk chair. Aaron breathed in the light floral scent—was it apples? "Thanks."

"What's this?" She nodded toward the document on the screen.

"Those are the ideas I had. They might not be any good." He lowered himself into the visitor chair and fought the urge to fidget while she read them over. He'd been brainstorming—truly—so had written down every idea that came without judgment. Should he explain that? Or was that talking for the sake of filling the air?

"Hmm." Holly's hand moved the mouse up and she highlighted several lines in the document. "I like these. This one in particular."

Aaron leaned forward to see better. If he got a noseful of apple again—and if that made his insides tighten—well, so be it. "The improvements pitch day?"

Holly nodded and glanced over her shoulder, smiling. "You listen when people talk, don't you?"

"I try." He was captured by her eyes and sinking fast. His gaze flicked down to her lips, then back up. Could she really not know what she did to him? "You said many of the developers had ideas—I figured other people might as well. And even if they didn't have an idea of their own, having the opportunity to weigh in and shape the direction of the app is only going to let people feel more invested."

"Which in turn will help them love their job. I think this is the one." Holly looked away and changed the highlight color on that item.

"You didn't have ideas? Maybe you have one that's better?" This was too fast. If they decided now, she'd make an excuse and leave. She'd been avoiding him since Monday afternoon—a tiny part of his mind registered that that was only two days. It probably made him pathetic. So be it.

Her shoulder lifted once. "I'll be honest. I didn't spend a lot of time thinking about it. Luca brought home a project that needed more parental participation than I prefer and it all got away from me."

"What was the project?"

She grunted. "He had to choose an aspect of the ancient Mali Empire and make a three-dimensional visual aid to explain it."

"Is that a fancy way to say a diorama?"

Holly chuckled. "Basically, yes. I think they've moved away from the term hoping that parents won't clue in. All I know is, his round hut is amazing, and I built more of it than he did."

Aaron wrinkled his nose. "Did he learn at least?"

"Oh, sure. He can regale you for hours about the Mali Empire. I don't think building the hut did anything to increase his knowledge and understanding, but maybe him turning it in will make the teacher feel like she did her job." Holly pinched the bridge of her nose. "That sounds catty. I know the teachers are working hard, and it's sure not a job I'd want, but I get irritated with homework that feels like busy work. We're plenty busy at home. I don't need school to help with that, you know?"

"I do." He blew out a breath and studied the list of ideas he'd had. "If you're sure about pitch day, let's go with it. We should hash out how to do it."

"What if we did it kind of like March madness?" Holly swiveled in her chair so her knees bumped his. She shifted and cut the contact. "Sorry. We could have a deadline say early next week for all the ideas—like a one paragraph write-up, nothing onerous. Then there could be a few days of voting and the best sixteen move into head-to-head competition."

How could he not admire a woman who got the thrill of

March madness? "I like it. Side question—do you like basketball?"

Her eyebrows lifted. "Who doesn't?"

Aaron grinned. "I'll make you a list. My name's not on it, by the way, but there are a lot of people out there who consider it a lesser sport."

"There are wrong people everywhere." She smiled and turned back to the computer. She opened a new document and started to type, outlining their conversation. "I think we should assign dates to everything today and try to kick off this week."

"Do we need to make sure Joe's on board first?"

Holly's forehead was scrunched when she turned to look at him. "Why?"

"Well. I guess to be sure he'll agree to move forward with the winner. I mean, if we have this whole contest to choose the next innovative addition to the platform, and then we don't follow through? We probably end up doing the opposite of getting people to love their job."

Holly snorted. "Okay. That's true. How do we do this, then?"

Aaron's knee bounced as he thought. They were unlikely to get in to see Joe any time soon. He was a busy man. Did they really need to see him? "Do you think we could just send an email? If we wrote up our proposal and sent it, that would be easier all around, right?"

"I think so. I'm a fan of email instead of meetings."

He winced. Was that a dig? He turned to look at her profile. Maybe not. "Okay, then it's like you said, let's write it up with deadlines and plans and all of that, but instead of moving forward this week, let's plan to have the first round next week so Joe has a couple of days to say yes or no."

"Should we copy Tyler on it?"

"Definitely." Aaron nodded, underscoring his words. "I can

only imagine how many emails Joe must get in an hour. This way, maybe Tyler can push for approval in a timely fashion."

"Sounds like a plan." Holly continued tapping at the keyboard.

Aaron scooted closer, reading over her shoulder and suggesting word tweaks here and there as she wrote it up. She had a great grasp of the concept—probably didn't need his input at all, except that they were a team, and he wanted to be part of it.

It took the better part of an hour before she leaned back and blew out a breath. "What do you think?"

"It's good. Let's send it."

Holly stood and gestured to the chair. "I'll let you do that. And then when you hear something, let me know?"

"Hang tight." Aaron changed chairs and switched to his email program. He opened a new message and addressed it to Joe and Tyler with a carbon copy to Holly. "Should I put urgent in the subject?"

"I wouldn't. That seems . . . excessive. Just mention that you'd like to know if it's a go by the end of the day Friday?"

"Yeah, all right." Aaron typed a quick intro and summary of their idea and attached the document Holly had typed up. "Sound good?"

"Yeah."

Aaron hit Send. "Do you want to grab dinner?"

"Oh. I should get home. Luca—"

"Probably also needs to eat dinner. I could grab burgers and bring them over."

"What are you doing, Aaron?" Holly inched backward until she bumped into the window. "I told you, I can't do this right now."

"Right now? Or ever?"

She frowned and looked away. "Realistically? Ever. Maybe

when Luca's out of the house, I'll be in a position to think about it."

"That's ten years. I don't want to wait that long."

Her eyes widened. "Aaron."

"I like you, Holly. I like Luca. I'm asking you to give me a chance. That's all. Just a chance. Maybe nothing will come from it, but wouldn't you like to know?"

Her head was shaking and her lips pressed together.

Aaron studied her and quietly let out a breath. "I'll let it go, but would you think about it? Please?"

"I'm not promising that. I have to go." Holly turned and practically ran from the room.

Aaron scrubbed his hands over his face. That could have gone better.

He reached for his phone and opened the group chat the guys in his Bible study used.

Anyone up for burgers? Maybe some Xbox at my place?

He set his phone aside and closed out all the programs on his laptop before shutting it down.

His phone pinged. Aaron glanced over and smiled. Ian.

I'm in if we can switch to pool or cards. I can't deal with anything video game related.

Aaron tapped out his response.

Works for me. Meet at 5Guys in twenty?

Deal.

Aaron nodded to himself and gathered up everything that needed to go home with him. The other guys might join them—at least they knew where and when if they decided to. And if not, an evening with Ian was always fun.

Although Ian's not wanting to play Xbox was concerning. The guy loved video games—it was why he was so good at his job.

Well, if something was wrong in Ian's world, Aaron would

find out over juicy grilled beef topped with bacon, mushrooms, and three kinds of cheese.

Between good food and conversation, maybe they'd both get the answers they were looking for.

~

"WHAT'S WRONG, BABY?" Holly slid a plate of spaghetti in front of Luca before carrying her plate to the spot across the table from him.

"Do I hafta eat salad?" Luca scowled at the bowl of lettuce smothered in ranch dressing that sat beside his plate.

"It barely qualifies as a vegetable at this point, so yes, you have to eat your ranch soup."

Luca's lips twitched, but his smile never completely surfaced. He sighed.

So. Not just the salad issue. Holly reached her hand across the table, palm up. "Let's pray."

Luca put his hand in hers but didn't curl his fingers. Holly squeezed his hand gently and closed her eyes, adding a silent plea for understanding and wisdom as she blessed the food.

"Did your teacher say anything about your hut?" She shook parmesan cheese out of the green container and pushed it across the table toward him.

He shrugged. "Three other kids made huts, too."

Of course, they had. What else were they supposed to make? Her first thought had been a spear, but obviously no one was going to actually make a weapon as a school project. Even if the teacher wanted to award a good grade, that would be overruled by the zero-tolerance policy for violence or the suggestion thereof. Given that Holly had gotten an email from Luca's teacher about his yelling "Hulk smash!" on the playground, a spear was an immediate no-go. "Well, the teacher can make a village then."

"I guess." He stabbed his fork into the noodles on his plate. "Do you think Mr. Powell likes me?"

Where had that come from? "I think so, yes. Why?"

"Would he come to my school Friday morning?"

What was Friday? Holly desperately searched her mind for whatever she'd forgotten. Field trip? No. "I don't—oh, honey."

"Donuts with Dad is lame."

Holly bit her lip. She'd been reprimanding him for saying "stupid" lately—apparently "lame" was his new replacement. But the broken look on his face left her unable to correct him. "I can come."

"You're my *mom*, not my dad." He shot her a look full of scorn. "And don't suggest Grandpa. I already asked him, and he's busy."

Drat her father. He was a fabulous grandfather—until he wasn't. "Did he say what he was doing?"

"No." Luca poked the noodles again. "I'm not hungry. Can I go watch TV?"

"No. You need to eat." Holly spun noodles around her fork and took a bite. Her own appetite had fled, but she could be a good example. "Let me call Grandpa and see if he can reschedule, okay?"

"I guess. I'd rather have Mr. Powell."

"How come?"

"Grandpa's old. He doesn't want to play the games. He eats his donut, makes sure I'm fine, and then leaves."

Holly frowned. "What do you mean he leaves? He doesn't stay for the program?"

Luca shook his head.

Fury ignited in her belly, and she slammed her fork down on the table.

Luca jolted.

"Sorry, baby. I'm not mad at you."

He nodded and scooped spaghetti noodles into his mouth. He slurped in the dangling noodle. "Can Mr. Powell come then?"

It was a big favor to ask of Aaron. Given their conversation in his office that afternoon, he'd probably say yes. But what strings would be attached to it? She didn't want to send the wrong impression—and anything that suggested she was letting him into her life outside of work was going to be the wrong impression. She hadn't lied that afternoon when she'd said she didn't have time for that. Luca was her priority.

And that right there was the crux of the issue.

Luca needed someone—a man, apparently—to go to Donuts with Dad. Someone not Holly's father. And boy, was she going to have words with Dad. Why hadn't Luca said something sooner? Probably because he loved his grandfather, warts and all. So did she, but that didn't mean he could ditch Luca for a golf game.

Holly picked up her fork and took another bite. "Is that all that's bothering you?"

"Seth says I don't have a dad because I'm a mutant."

"Seth says that, does he?" Apparently, Holly was going to be texting Seth's mom this evening, in addition to calling her father. "And what do you think about that?"

"I think he's a mutant."

She fought a smile. Definitely the wrong response. "Let's not call names just because he started it."

Luca jerked a shoulder.

She sighed. "You have a father, honey. He's just not part of our lives. I'm sorry that it's hard for you."

"Is it hard for you, too?"

She closed her eyes and nodded once. "Sometimes. But we do okay, don't we?"

"We'd do okayer if I didn't have to eat salad."

Holly laughed. "Tell you what. Why don't you eat half of the salad, and we'll see what happens."

"Okay. I love you, Mom."

"I love you, too." She looked down at her barely touched dinner and nudged it away. She wasn't going to be able to choke it down, no matter how much she told Luca he needed to eat his. Hopefully, tonight wouldn't be one of the nights where he called out all her hypocritical parenting decisions. "I'm going to go call Grandpa, okay? You eat."

"If he comes, he has to stay. And let me get the jelly-filled one."

She smiled. "I'll tell him."

"K."

Holly stood, kissed the top of his head, and padded into her bedroom. She shut the door and took her cell phone off the charger. Was there anyone else she could ask? A couple of men at church came to mind, but she discarded them just as quickly. With a sigh, she perched on the edge of her bed and tapped her parents' contact.

"Hi, Holly. How are you, dear?"

"I'm good, Mom. Is Dad there?"

"Sure. He's right here—you're on speaker."

Of course she was. Mom always put the phone on speaker. That explained the drone of the TV in the background. "Hi, Dad."

He might have grunted, Holly wasn't sure. It was still probably all she was going to get if he was watching something. She cleared her throat. "Donuts with Dad is Friday. The timing got away from me—sorry for the late notice."

"Oh. This week?" Dad coughed and the TV noise disappeared. He must have muted it. "I have an early tee time with Frank and Arlow. What time is it?"

"Seven thirty. For an hour. A *whole* hour."

Dad cleared his throat. "Told you about that, did he?"

"Yes, Dad, he did. But it took him nearly a year. What were you thinking? This is your grandson."

"I know, I know. Look, if it helps, your mother already ripped into me about it."

"That's true, I did. Maybe I need to again. Your daughter's right—Luca is your grandson, and I expect more from you." Mom sighed. "Honestly, I'm so ashamed of you I can hardly take it."

Holly smiled slightly at her mom's drama. "So, Friday?"

"I can't. I'm sorry. It's quite a drive to get up there now, and I'd need to leave early. Plus, I can't reschedule the game again."

"I could go." Mom's voice was overly bright. "I know I'm not a dad, but then neither is your father."

"Well, he's my dad, but I hear what you're saying." Holly sighed. "Don't worry about it, Mom. I'll figure something out."

"Why don't you two come down for the weekend? The weather's supposed to warm up a little. We could go for a walk on the beach."

"Thanks, Mom. I'll let you know."

"Which means no, thank you. It's fine."

"I'm sorry. It's just—"

"You don't owe us an explanation. You're busy and you have your own life and we're proud of you."

Her mother's words warmed Holly. Sometimes, she wasn't sure that Mom actually understood. Or had forgiven her for being a single mom in the first place. "Thanks. Love you guys."

She ended the call and stared at her phone. Luca wanted Aaron. He was a better option than anyone else she could come up with. With a twisting stomach, she tapped Aaron's contact and waited as it rang.

"Holly? Everything okay?"

She closed her eyes. He was a good man. "I'm fine. We're fine. I actually have kind of a huge favor to ask you."

"Me?"

Based on the incredulity in his voice, Holly could picture his face. She'd seen that expression a few times at work. "You. It's a big ask and you're free to say no. No harm done, no hard feelings. I promise."

"You're scaring me a little. Just ask."

"Luca's school does a thing every year, and my dad usually goes, but the date got away from me this year, so he can't make it. Plus, they moved to Hampton so they're not just across town anymore, which makes it trickier. And really, you can say no. I realize—"

"Holly. Spit it out."

Her laugh was high and thin and full of nerves. "Sorry. Donuts and dads. It's on Friday at seven thirty. It lasts an hour. I realize we'd need to move our meeting, and that's fine with me. Luca specifically asked if you could join him."

Holly held her breath.

"Donuts? I'm in."

"Just like that?" She breathed out in a whoosh.

"Well, maybe now that you mention it, I have a condition."

Dang it. She should have just said thank you. "Okay?"

"Let me take you and Luca to dinner Friday night."

"Aaron." She stopped and took a deep breath. "I knew I shouldn't have asked you to do this, but Luca brought you up, and my dad is flaking out, but can't you see that this isn't going to work?"

"Not really. I can see you're scared—or at least I think that's what I'm seeing. But I like you. You're smart and funny. You're a great mom. Luca's a fun kid. And I can't stop thinking about what it might be like to kiss you. I'd like to take you to dinner. That's it. Give me a chance? Please?"

She couldn't say she hadn't thought about what it might be like to kiss Aaron, but she also knew that kisses weren't the most important thing in the world. "I . . . "

Holly bit her lip. She should say no. She could ask Landon to do the donut thing. Not that he wouldn't take it as encouragement, too. And Luca . . . Luca wanted Aaron. "All right. Dinner. I can't promise more than that."

"That's okay. We can take it as it comes. You want to text me the details on the donut thing?"

"I'll do that now. Thanks, Aaron. This means a lot to Luca."

"Just to Luca?"

"No. Not just him." It was too much of an admission. It was giving him hope she had no right to offer. But she couldn't stop herself from dreaming, at least a little. It could never be reality. In her heart, she knew that. Just like she knew the dream would hurt when it ended.

But in the meantime? She didn't want to let it go.

7

Holly watched the clock in the corner of her computer screen as she worked. Donuts with Dad should be over. How had it gone? There was no reason to expect it to have gone poorly—Aaron was a nice guy. Luca and he got along. The school had been understanding of the last-minute addition.

And yet, her stomach still twisted.

Dinner tonight.

Luca was over the moon. He was already angling to turn it into another movie night with Aaron. And it was hard to steel herself enough to say no. It made sense to continue with Marvel movies—particularly if Hulk involvement was an option. Should she just offer to cook?

"Hey."

She jolted a little and spun in her chair. He'd dressed down —dark jeans and a sweater with a mock turtleneck collar and a zipper in the front. She swallowed. Why did he have to look so good? "How'd it go?"

"It was fun. Luca and I both got a jelly donut out of it—and he was begging for a second one when they said it was time for us to go. I'm not sure if his teacher was going to fall for it or not."

Holly sighed. That boy. "He has a big sweet tooth."

"I noticed. He conned me out of close to half of mine because he wanted to try it."

"Oh, no." She covered her face. "I'm sorry."

"Hey, it's fine. I thought it was funny. Anyway, he'll be on a sugar high until lunch."

"At least." She shook her head. Those poor teachers. "I think today is a PE day. That should help some."

He chuckled. "Do you have time to meet? I saw an email from Tyler in my inbox. Hopefully it's the go ahead."

She turned back to her computer and wiggled her mouse, then opened her email. "I have it too. Should we look?"

"Duh." He grinned. "They have to say yes, don't they?"

"No one ever *has* to say yes." She trapped her lower lip between her teeth and clicked on the email. She scanned the note and her cheeks heated. "They think it's a good idea."

"And they appreciated the full write-up." Aaron put his hand on her shoulder and the warmth seemed to soak into her heart. "That was you."

"You helped." She glanced up at him over her shoulder. He was closer than she'd realized. Holly moistened her lips. "We should get together and hash out how we're going to announce it to the crew and track things."

"I was thinking we could use the internal version of Social. I poked around—it looked easy enough to add the bracket system to the voting mechanism."

His eyes had little yellow rings around their pupils. She'd never been close enough to notice and now she couldn't look away. "What?"

His lips quirked. "The internal voting mechanism?"

"Oh." Holly blinked. *Get your head in the game, Holl.* "That's a great idea. I've done custom versions of that before—you're right. It's definitely doable."

Aaron straightened, but his hand remained on her shoulder. She couldn't convince herself to nudge it off. She liked it. He cleared his throat. "If you can set the technical part up, I can do all the writing and shoot out a blast when it's ready."

Holly nodded. "Easy. Maybe even by tonight—Monday at the end of the day for sure."

"That fast?"

"Yeah. Like I said, I've coded in there before—I can already see how it needs to go. I'll send you links when I've got the basic interface ready and you can start plugging in the instructions." She turned back to the computer and scanned the email again. "They were even good with our original dates."

"Then we're good to go." Aaron patted her shoulder then tucked his hands into his pockets.

"I guess we are." She grinned up at him. She'd been excited about the idea on Wednesday, but waiting for Joe and Tyler to chime in—plus the donut thing—had dampened it some. Now it was back. She cocked her head to the side and studied Aaron. "Luca's hoping you'll watch another movie after dinner tonight."

"He mentioned it once or twice. I told him we had to wait to see what his mom said."

Holly pressed her lips together a moment before smiling. "His mom was kind of hoping you'd stay, too."

"Then I can't wait." His grin arrowed straight into her heart. Maybe it was stupid. Maybe it wouldn't last.

But maybe just this once she deserved a chance to be happy.

AARON READ over the email he'd drafted to tell the Social team about the Betterment Brackets—the name was cutesy, but Holly said it was fun, so they'd go with it. It had all the information they needed. It was enthusiastic. And it contained links for the internal version of Social where all the different levels of the competition would take place.

He shot it over to Holly for one final look before it would get blasted out to everyone, then tapped out a text to ask her to look right away.

His phone rang. "This is Aaron."

"Did you seriously just text me about an email?" Holly's voice held suppressed laughter.

Heat seared his cheeks. "I wasn't sure how busy you were."

"I guess that makes sense. It's still hilarious."

"Glad I can provide amusement. Although, I guess I'm going to go ahead and point out that you called me because I texted you about an email." He shook his head, but his lips twitched. "Let me know if we need to tweak it."

"Hang on. I'm reading it now."

Aaron fought the urge to fidget. There was no reason he couldn't—she was across the building in her cube, and he was in his office. But it still seemed like she'd know. The seconds ticked by. Shouldn't she have something to say?

"It's good. No tweaks."

He blew out a breath. "You're sure?"

"I'm sure. Get it out, and people can read it before they go home for the weekend. Then they can think about what they want to submit."

"You don't think we should wait until Monday morning? What about people who've already left? Does including some of the weekend give an unfair advantage?"

"Nope. I don't think so. Everyone I know has their work email on their phone and at least checks the subject line when something comes in. So make the subject intriguing."

He laughed. "Oh, sure. No pressure."

"None at all. I'm sure you'll be fine. I've got to run in about five so I can pick up Luca. We'll meet you at the restaurant?"

"You don't want me to pick you up?" He'd been banking on that. More time together. And it felt more like a date. Maybe that was the problem.

"Oh. Well. I just thought it would be easier. Um ..."

"It's okay. I'll meet you there. You're probably right that it's easier. I'm just looking forward to tonight."

She cleared her throat, but that was the only response for what felt like too long. Then finally said, "Me, too."

He grinned. "Great. Six still good?"

"Six. Bye."

Aaron stared at his email program. He needed a compelling subject line. Something that was going to get everyone to open —and not just open, be excited about the contest inside. For a moment, doubt settled on him like a cloak of lead. Was asking people to help them improve their app really a way to get them to love their jobs?

Holly had said there were many features and improvements that got brought up. He'd seen the lack of follow-through himself. And he had big clients who frequently mentioned that it would be nice if such-and-such feature were available. If he was able to suggest a change and then see it through to completion, how would that affect his feelings about his job?

Aaron's head bobbed from side to side as he considered. Then he nodded. Yeah, she was right—seemed like Holly was always right. They were definitely on the right track.

He added the email alias that would send the message to everyone in their branch of Robinson Enterprises, put in a subject line, shot up a quick prayer that this wasn't a terrible idea, and hit Send.

There was nothing more to do about this tonight. In fact, there wouldn't be anything to do until next Friday night after the open submission period for the first round ended. Which meant he could focus on Holly now. And Luca.

He grinned.

Luca was a gem. He didn't suffer from being raised by a single mom—not that Aaron had really expected that. Not with Holly as his mom. Still, this morning had been a fascinating and delightful experience. They'd laughed almost the entire time. Aaron was looking forward to spending more time with Luca tonight. Almost as much as he was excited to see Holly outside of work.

He gathered his laptop, some files for clients who tended to reach out on the weekends with questions, and his coat. It was a quick trip down to his car, and not much longer to the burger restaurant where he'd arranged to meet Holly and Luca.

Under normal circumstances, it wasn't the kind of place he'd go for a first date. None of this was normal. He'd never dated a single mom. He'd never been half in love with someone before finally convincing them to go out with him.

And he'd never suspected that a child was his son.

"There he is!" Near the door, Luca danced in place.

Holly held him by the hand, her face in shadows.

"Am I late?"

"No. Someone was excited." Holly stepped out from under the awning so her face was visible. "So we came straight here from the sitter."

"Mom. She's not a babysitter." Luca growled in the back of his throat. "It's afterschool club."

"Oh, so sorry." Holly's eyes sparkled with laughter as she shifted her gaze up to meet Aaron's. "You'll have to excuse me. I forgot that Luca's too old for a babysitter."

Aaron's lips curved.

"I'm not a baby!"

Holly ruffled Luca's hair. "You're *my* baby."

Luca made gagging noises and danced out of Holly's reach.

Aaron laughed. "Scamp. Hungry?"

"Starving. They wouldn't let us have another donut before class." Luca slipped his hand into Aaron's and tipped his head up, eyes wide. "Can you believe it?"

Given how many donuts the kids around them had been scarfing down, Aaron definitely could believe it. He savored the warmth of Luca's small hand in his as he reached for the restaurant door with his other hand. "So unfair."

Holly snickered and drilled a finger into Luca's belly. "How many donuts did you get?"

"Only four."

"Uh-huh. Only."

"Four?" Aaron looked down at the boy and shook his head. "Who'd you con out of another donut?"

Luca grinned and scooted through the door to stand by Holly. "My friend Greg didn't like his."

Shaking his head, Aaron closed the distance between himself and Holly and placed one hand on her shoulder. She stiffened, then relaxed.

He wasn't going to take it personally. This was new—for both of them. They navigated the ordering process at the counter, with Luca angling for extras at every turn and Holly shutting most of them down. She'd tried to pay for theirs, and then it had been Aaron's turn to shut things down. At least her protest hadn't been much more than a token.

And it had been his pleasure to add milkshakes for each of them to the order.

When dinner was over, they tossed their trash.

"Can Mr. Aaron come watch a movie, Mom? Can he?" Luca turned his gaze on Aaron. "Can you?"

"If your mom's still good with it, I am." Aaron looked over at Holly, eyebrows lifted. "Still okay?"

"Yeah." Holly nodded and held out her hand to Luca. "We'll meet you at home."

"Can I ride in his car?" Luca's pleading gaze turned back on Holly.

"Oh. Well. I don't know if Aaron—"

"Maybe next time, okay bud? I think maybe I should drive your mom somewhere first, so she knows I'm a safe driver." Aaron smiled slightly and looked at Holly. "Maybe I could pick the two of you up for church on Sunday?"

Holly's eyes widened. "But you don't go to Cornerstone."

"Do they allow visitors?"

The edges of her laugh were tinged with nerves. "Of course, they do."

"Then it'll be fine. We can work out the details after the movie." Aaron ruffled Luca's hair. "Let's get going. I'm excited to see Hulk smash some more."

"Smash!" Luca flexed like the green superhero before giggling like a loon.

"C'mon, Kid Hulk. Let's get going." Her gaze flicked up and latched with his. "We'll see you there."

Aaron followed them to the parking lot and waited while they got settled in Holly's car before heading to his own.

It was good the night wasn't over yet—he wasn't ready to let go.

8

Luca was waiting in the doorway of Holly's townhouse when Aaron turned into the visitor parking spot right in front of their house.

"He's here!" Luca disappeared back inside the house.

Aaron chuckled, made his way up the path to the door, and knocked.

Holly padded barefoot from the back of the house where he knew the kitchen was. "Come on in. Luca told the whole neighborhood you were here."

"I heard. I didn't want to presume." He stepped in and shut the door behind himself. "Is Luca getting the movie ready?"

"Yeah, he's downstairs."

"Do you need me to take anything down?"

Holly shook her head. "I'm just fixing lemonade and some popcorn. Luca insisted that we had to have it, even though I'm stuffed."

He remembered being a bottomless pit when he was little. "Boys like to eat."

"Tell me. I'm terrified of what's going to happen when he's a teenager. Go on down. I'll be there in a minute."

Aaron wanted to stay there with Holly—he had a mental image of leaning against the counter and watching as she moved around the kitchen. She was efficient—definitely not flirty—so why was he so drawn to her?

Her eyebrows lifted.

Right. Mental picture or not, he was better off downstairs with Luca. At least there, he knew he'd be welcomed with open arms.

Aaron slipped out of his shoes, leaving them near the door, and headed to the stairs. He jogged down to the open area Holly called the rec room. A large TV held court on the long wall. A sofa and some beanbags were arranged in a loose semi-circle in front of it. Outside of the TV area, there was a four-person felt-covered table with chairs. There was a foosball table in a corner. And on the other side of the room, an elliptical and small selection of free weights.

"Are you ready? Have you seen this one? It's great! Hulk climbs a building and grabs the big alien spaceship and *smashes* it." Luca dove into to the beanbags he'd stacked on top of one another.

Aaron grinned. "Let's wait for your mom—we don't want her to miss anything."

"Okay. You can sit down here with me if you want." Luca patted one of the beanbags.

He wanted to sit with Holly on the couch. Maybe find an excuse to slide his arm around her shoulders. But there was time for that. For all he knew, she wouldn't even be open to it. She'd agreed to dinner—and it felt like maybe she was opening up to the idea of more—but it was better not to push. "Sounds like a plan."

Aaron grabbed the beanbag chair and fluffed it before settling in. It wasn't *un*comfortable, but he wasn't going to be changing over his seating at home any time soon.

Luca scooted another beanbag close and plopped into it, resting his head on Aaron's shoulder. His heart melted. This kid.

"Tell me about your day. What happened after donut time?" Aaron adjusted his position slightly.

Luca sighed. "We had reading first. I hate reading."

"How come?"

"It's hard. And the kids laugh at me because I'm slow. I can read. I'm not a baby."

"Never doubted it. Do the letters wiggle around?"

Luca twisted his head up so his wide eyes locked on Aaron's. "Do they do that to you, too?"

"If I don't concentrate. Do some of them look the same?"

"Yes. And the other kids call me a baby."

Aaron's heart broke. "Have you told your mom? Or the teacher?"

"I tried to tell the teacher. She said if I sat still, the letters wouldn't move." He shrugged. "Mom has to work. What's she going to do?"

"Can I tell your mom?"

"If you want." He waited a minute, his fingers twisting together in his lap. "You don't think I'm a baby?"

"Nope. I think you need to do some testing so they can figure out the best way to help you with your reading. What happened after reading time?"

"Math. I like it okay. We're learning long division. Did you know you could have stuff left over?"

"Remainders, right? Pretty advanced stuff. I didn't realize you were a math genius."

Luca preened a little. "Then we had PE and lunch and it was a history day. We started a new unit on Greece. Did you know they all wore dumb-looking dresses?"

"I've heard that."

"Do we call things dumb?" Holly handed them a bowl of popcorn and fixed Luca with a glare.

He hunched his shoulder. "No, ma'am. But have you seen them?"

"I have. And while I also prefer modern fashion, I think we should go ahead and not name call." Holly settled onto the sofa with a smaller bowl of popcorn. "There's lemonade over on the table if you get thirsty."

"Can't I drink it here?" Luca turned a pleading gaze on Holly.

"Nope. Hit Play." She tapped Aaron's shoulder. "You can sit up here if you'd rather. I know the floor isn't the best."

Aaron watched Luca scramble to the DVD player and push the button before he crawled back and wiggled a new wallow into the beanbag. His head, once again, dropped onto Aaron's shoulder.

"I'm good."

Holly's steady gaze did crazy things to his heart. Finally, she nodded. "Okay."

"Shh. You have to pay attention." Luca slipped his hand into Aaron's. Aaron swallowed and focused on the screen. This felt right. Like a little family.

He glanced down at Luca, his heart already lost. Even if nothing worked out between him and Holly, Aaron was going to do what he could to stay in the boy's life. Every kid needed some kind of male role model, didn't they? Would Holly let him step into that role?

By the time the battle of New York was raging on the screen, Luca had fallen asleep. Holly didn't look like she was that far behind him.

"Do you want to stop it? I can take Luca to his room and let you both get some sleep."

Holly blinked. "I'm awake."

Aaron chuckled. "Barely. Luca isn't. Can I carry him for you?"

"Oh. Well." She bit her lip. "It's probably easier to wake him. He has to brush his teeth and get his pjs on. All of that. But thanks."

He thought about arguing, but he didn't exactly have the standing to do that. "Okay."

"Luca, baby. Wake up and go get ready for bed." Holly rubbed Luca's shoulder.

He stirred and grunted.

Holly shook her head. "He's always been a heavy sleeper." She stood and tugged him into her arms. "Come on, honey. Bedtime."

"K." Luca's head rolled around before dropping onto Holly's shoulder.

She staggered a step.

Aaron pushed quickly to his feet. "Do you want me to get him? I can at least carry him up. Maybe when he's in his room it'll be easier to get him to wake?"

"I probably have him." She hitched him higher then blew out a breath. "But if you're sure you don't mind, I guess it beats breaking my back."

Aaron fought a grin and reached for the boy. He met Holly's gaze. "Thank you."

"I think that's my line." She cleared her throat. "It's all the way upstairs. You're sure you have him?"

"I'm sure. Lead on." Aaron's heart was full. Was it just having an armful of sleeping child? Would any child feel the same way? Or was it specific to this boy . . . and his mom? He followed Holly up the stairs, then paused for a moment on the main floor before continuing up to the next level.

Holly stood in a small room that had been painted pale green. Posters of superheroes—primarily Hulk, but there were others featured, too—decorated the walls. A toy chest spilled over with action figures, trucks, and dinosaurs. She gestured to the bottom bunk. "Just set him there. If I need to, I can get him ready without him being alert. He won't love it in the morning, but he'll deal."

"Okay." Aaron lowered Luca to the bed and stepped back, tucking his hands in his pockets. "I guess I'll let you get to that. Thanks for coming to dinner with me."

She smiled slightly. "I'll walk you down. He's not going anywhere."

"Okay." *Lame. Don't you know anything else to say?* But he didn't. He didn't want to leave, but Holly was clearly not going to ask him to stay. He followed her down to the main floor.

She clasped her hands at her waist in the middle of the foyer. "I had a lovely evening. So did Luca. I hope you're not upset that he fell asleep. It's a lot past his bedtime."

"It's all good. I had fun, too. Luca's great. He mentioned something about reading and I wanted to ask if you'd ever considered that he might have dyslexia."

She shook her head. "I've got an appointment with the eye doctor—I noticed he was squinting. I figured he just needed glasses."

"It's possible. But if that doesn't fix it, it's worth exploring. He said the letters wiggle and look the same a lot."

"Oh." She frowned. "That doesn't sound like blurry vision. Why do you think dyslexia based on that?"

"I'm dyslexic, so it was familiar."

"I'll talk to his teacher. Thanks."

"You're welcome." He cocked his head to the side, watching her. "What time should I pick you up for church?"

"You don't have to do that. I didn't think—"

"I'd really like to join you. I can meet you there if that makes you more comfortable."

"Oh." Holly looked everywhere but at his face. Her cheeks burned dark pink.

Aaron eased closer. He reached up to gently brush a strand of hair off her forehead and tuck it back behind her ear. He left his hand there, cupping her cheek. "Holly."

She met his gaze. Her eyes were a sea of confused longing. It was all the invitation he needed.

Aaron leaned closer, slowly. If she backed away, he'd let her. His lips met hers. Warm and soft. She made a sound that was half whimper and half . . . what? He started to ease back but her hands slid up his chest and curved around his neck. Her fingers wove through his hair and her mouth fastened on his, full of heat and impatience.

Aaron lost himself in the kiss. His hands drifted down to her shoulders.

Holly broke away and stumbled back two steps, her hands flying to her mouth. "Oh, no. I'm so sorry."

He rubbed his lips together, savoring the memory of her exuberance. "Do I look upset?"

"No." She shook her head. "I guess you don't. It's just been a long time."

He smiled slightly. "For me, too."

"Oh, please. I'm sure women are throwing themselves at your feet."

"Doesn't mean I'm picking them up and dusting them off. Holly, I—"

"Mom?" Luca's sleepy voice traveled down from his bedroom.

Holly held up a finger and turned to look over her shoulder. "I'll be right there, baby. Get some jammies on, okay?"

"K. Did Mr. Aaron leave?"

"Not quite yet. He's on his way though." Holly mouthed *sorry*.

"Oh. Bye Mr. Aaron."

"Bye, Luca. I'll see you at church, okay?"

"Okay!"

"You're serious about the church thing, aren't you?"

"I'm serious about you." Aaron took a step forward and reached out to lightly touch her arm. "That kiss? I've been wanting to do that for a while. I'd really like to do it again."

"Oh." Holly blinked. "Um . . ."

"Maybe we can talk about it later. You could call me after you get Luca settled."

"Call you?"

"Sure. On the phone. You have my number." She looked dazed. Confused. And scared. "Think about it. Either way, I'll see you Sunday morning. I'll just look the church up online and text you about the pickup time."

"Eight thirty." Holly blew out a breath. "We usually leave at eight thirty."

He grinned and it felt as though everything inside of him settled. Maybe she wasn't pushing him off completely. "I'll get going."

It took everything he had not to cross to where she stood at the foot of the stairs and pull her back into his arms for another kiss. If anyone was keeping score, he wanted points for that.

He stepped out onto her porch, then checked that the door was completely closed before heading to his car. The chill in the air cooled his body, but it was going to take longer for his mind to follow.

Hopefully, she'd call him.

Despite it being the right choice to leave, he wasn't ready for their evening to end.

∼

"READY?" Aaron rubbed Holly's shoulders as she ran the vote tabulation on the two matchups of the final four improvement ideas.

The contest had been running for two weeks and it was scheduled to end on Friday. They'd announce the final two today. There'd be presentations on Wednesday and the final votes would close out at five on Thursday afternoon. The winner would be announced on Friday—just squeaking in on the requirement for the entire event to happen during February.

Holly looked over her shoulder and met Aaron's gaze.

They'd been dating—officially—for two weeks, too. But that wasn't scheduled to end anytime soon. At least, she hoped not. "Here we go."

"Oh, wow." Aaron pointed to one of the matchups. "What are the chances that there would be a tie?"

"I mean, it's not unheard of."

"Don't actually do the math, okay?" He winked.

Her insides turned to mush. He had a tendency to do that to her. Her cheeks heated. "Right. We did plan for that in our rules."

"We did?" His eyebrows lifted.

Holly chuckled. "Go us? If there's a tie, we get to decide."

"Oh." Aaron frowned. "That's . . . a lot of pressure."

"More pressure than sneaking in a satisfying kiss when a certain nine-year-old runs to the bathroom on Friday movie night?"

"Nothing is higher pressure than that. Except maybe this." He straightened and looked over the top of the cube farm, then leaned in and pressed his lips to hers. There was nothing perfunctory about it, either. When Aaron kissed her? He was focused.

"Ahem."

Holly broke the kiss. Her face was hot—probably also red as

a tomato. She looked over and wanted to crawl into a hole. "Hi, Tyler."

He smirked. "I thought I'd come see what the final two improvements were going to be. I didn't mean to interrupt."

Aaron shook his head. "That's why you interrupted, I guess?"

"Aaron." Holly glared at him.

Tyler laughed. "Got me there. I couldn't help myself. It's nice to see teams figure out how to work together."

"I don't imagine this is what you had in mind." Holly turned back to her computer. "Anyway, we have a tie. The rules we published said we get to choose—but maybe you'd like to do the honors?"

"Oh no, I'm an impartial observer." Tyler stepped closer and studied the screen. "That's a tough choice. What was the other matchup?"

Holly scrolled down so that one was visible. "The winner here doesn't have a huge margin."

"I can see that." Tyler tapped a finger on his lip. "I wonder if you have time to do a rematch? Pair them up the other way and see if you get a definitive winner."

"Hmm." Holly glanced at Aaron. He didn't have an obvious expression of distaste at the idea. But he also wasn't cheering for joy. "What do you think?"

Aaron shrugged. "We could do it, but it'd have to be today only. The winners need time to work on their presentations."

If they were smart, the people whose ideas went into the final four should have started on their presentations. Worst case, they wouldn't need it, but Holly would never have waited until she only had two days to give a presentation on an idea that could go into production. "Should we see if they've already started? If they haven't, then maybe we choose a winner. If they have, losing one day won't be as big a deal. And I can stay and declare the winners tonight—and email them. That way they haven't lost much at all."

Tyler was nodding. "I like that better than you two making an arbitrary choice."

"It wouldn't be arbitrary, but I understand what you're saying." Aaron frowned slightly. "Okay. Let's do that. How long will it take to set up?"

Holly tapped a few keys and the new matchups displayed. She double-checked the closing time on the poll and published it. "About that long."

"It's ready?" Aaron smiled. "You're amazing."

Her cheeks heated. "It's the program—I didn't do anything. I can send out an email blast and let people know that, because they were so close, we're trying it this way. What happens if there's another tie? Or two ties this time?"

Tyler laughed. "If that happens, then flip a coin. But don't lose those other ideas, because it sounds like they're probably worthwhile, too."

"I already saved them off to a future releases file." Holly hunched her shoulders. "They are good ideas. Honestly, all of the ideas that made the top eight are worth keeping around."

"I saved them, too." Aaron chuckled. "And made a note that future improvements need to have support like this. All our employees are active on Social—if they don't like or see the need? Then it's probably not a feature we should be sinking time into."

"Eh. Maybe. Maybe not. Sometimes the power users miss something that a more casual user would actually enjoy. Don't rule out user suggestions or even the importance of keeping an eye on the competition."

Those were valid points. Holly nodded. She'd been drafting the all-hands email while Tyler spoke. She read it over a second time, then scooted so Aaron could see. "Does that work?"

Aaron leaned in. His lips brushed her ear and she fought a shiver. "That looks good. Send it."

"Let me know the final two, would you?" Tyler knocked on the metal edge of her cube walls. "See you later."

Holly listened to the receding footsteps as they faded away. She blew out a breath. "Do you think he's checking up on everyone like that?"

"More than likely, yeah. He said in that first meeting that he would. Joe, too."

He had? Holly thought back and tried to bring up a memory of that, then shrugged. If Aaron said it, he was probably right. He had good recall. In fact, he'd mentioned a few things that had started her thinking it was possible the two of them had met in college. She veered away from that train of thought—it kept her up at night filled with mortification, and she didn't need it intruding on work hours, too. "Seems like we passed?"

"I think so." Aaron rubbed her shoulder. "I'm also pretty sure he's okay with relationships developing between the teammates. Maybe it was even part of the design."

"What? No way." Holly shook her head. She just didn't want to picture Joe and Tyler putting their heads together to try and play matchmaker. "Why would they do that?"

"I don't know. And I could be wrong—it wasn't my thought originally. I overheard Melanie—she's on the game team—saying something along those lines. I don't think it's too far out in left field."

"I do." Holly crossed her arms. "They don't know any of us well enough to decide who we'd pair up with. So we work together, so what? That's not a guarantee of anything."

Aaron held up his hands, his eyebrows lifting. "Okay. Sorry."

She pinched the bridge of her nose. "No, I'm sorry. I don't like the idea that someone's meddling in my life. Or that I don't have a choice in something."

"You have a choice, Holl." He waited until she looked up and met his gaze. "You always have a choice with me."

His eyes were clouded. Had she hurt him? "I didn't mean to hurt your feelings. I like this thing between us. I like where it's heading."

"Even if we were pushed together by Joe and Tyler?"

"Even if." She forced her lips to curve. Hopefully they hadn't been, though. How was that any different than her friends dragging her to a party and cajoling her to drink? And keep drinking. And then disappearing and leaving her alone with some guy whose face she could never bring into focus. Now she had Luca, and he was her world, but what would her life have been if she hadn't had to pivot into single-mom land?

"You okay?"

Holly took in the concern evident on Aaron's face and nodded, firmly shutting the door on unproductive ruminations. "Yeah. Of course. Sorry."

"You're sure?"

"Totally sure. You should get to work, though. And so should I."

He looked like he was going to say more, but he only gave a slight shake of his head. "What if I came by at the end of the day to check winners and email them with you?"

"I'd like that." She forced her smile to brighten. "Oh. Shoot. We sent out that email without checking on the presentation status. What if they haven't started on them yet?"

"I'll swing by and touch base with the four of them and let you know. I think they still have enough time—it's not like they'd be working on their presentation during work hours anyway. Or, if they were going to, not like they can't start doing that even if they end up not needing to present." He shrugged.

"Okay. Let me know?" Not like she could do anything about it. The poll was live and the email had been sent out. And—she switched over to check, and gave a short laugh—people were already voting.

"I will." Aaron leaned in and kissed her forehead. "Don't stress out, okay? It's going to be fine."

"Right. Of course, it is."

He chuckled as he left her cube.

Holly buried her face in her hands. What was wrong with her? Always worrying about things before they were actual problems. Borrowing trouble, that was what her mother called it. Except, she'd had a bad feeling about going to that party in college and still let herself be talked into it. And now she had that same, sick sense of foreboding in her stomach.

She'd keep praying for clarity—something she hadn't done in college—and hopefully God would tell her what to do. She didn't want to break things off with Aaron. She wanted to believe he was the man God had for her. That being with him— marrying him and letting him be a dad to Luca—was God's will.

But she also couldn't—wouldn't—risk it if she wasn't sure.

Right now, she wasn't sure about anything anymore.

9

In the passenger seat, Holly watched Aaron from the side of her eye as he backed out of the church parking lot. This was the sixth week he'd showed up to collect them and joined them at Cornerstone. It was probably safe to say he wasn't attending the megachurch anymore. But a part of her shied away from embracing that. "Do you miss your church?"

He glanced over, puzzled. "Not really. I still have Monday night Bible study with the guys—and that was the majority of the connection I had there. Pastor Brown is a great preacher, but so is the pastor here. And I like being with you."

"And me!" Luca waved his hands between the seats. "Right?"

Aaron laughed. "Of course."

"I just don't like thinking you gave up something you loved because you wanted to spend time with me."

"I wouldn't say I loved it. Or that I gave it up. I'm still going to church, still enjoying church, still being challenged in my faith and encouraged to grow. If anything, this move has been good for me, because I have to be purposeful about attending. It's no longer a convenient something to do on Saturday night."

"See? That's just it. You liked to sleep in, and I took that away from you."

He shrugged. "It's not a big loss. And I still get to sleep in most Saturdays. Plus, I usually go home after lunch and take a nap. I'm not sleep deprived."

"But—"

"What's going on, Hol?"

She frowned and glanced into the back seat, where Luca was bopping back and forth to the music. "I guess I just don't want you to feel obligated to do church with us. It's not like we're your family."

His eyebrows lifted.

Holly winced. "I didn't mean—I just—you know what, never mind."

"Don't do that. Go ahead and tell me what you're thinking."

The problem, of course, was that she wasn't sure what she was thinking. She'd been itchy all morning—longer, really—since the night before? The week before? Aaron was everywhere she turned. He was there at work, leaving his office to swing by and say hi, or cajole her into eating lunch out when she had a perfectly good PB&J in her desk drawer. He was taking her and Luca out to eat on Fridays, or having them over and grilling, or coming to her house for whatever she had on the menu. He was at the grocery store. He picked them up for church and stayed for lunch.

And Luca. Every other word out of Luca's mouth, it seemed, was "Mr. Aaron." He was anxious to do a video call after school to tell Aaron about a test grade or a project or something silly that happened on the playground.

Six weeks in, and Aaron was this deeply rooted part of her life—their life—and she didn't have the experience to support the idea that he'd really want to stay. Not for long.

"I can be. I'm not managing to pass this cartel mission fast enough, so the dumb bombs keep exploding before I'm far enough away."

Aaron nodded. "You remember I quit playing that game because of that?"

"Nope. I'd forgotten that completely. Smarter than I am, it seems."

"I could've told you that a long time ago."

Ian laughed. "Dream on. You loaded up?"

"Yep. Let's do this." Aaron watched the cut scene as it started to play, introducing the virus that created the zombies and stranded people around the globe.

Ian growled. "I wish they'd let us skip these."

Aaron hissed out a breath as the opening ended and a zombie lunged from the shadows. "Where do they hide the weapons in this game?"

"There's a cache over here by me."

Aaron worked to get his character over to where Ian's was. There were a few weapons, but not many. Had this game always been like that? He'd taken a break for a while—maybe this was why. "Got it. Let's do that first mission."

"Okay. Head toward the first waypoint. Aw, man. I died."

Aaron grunted and sifted through his inventory for a medkit that would revive Ian's character. "You're up."

"Thanks, man. So. You and Holly? What's going on?" Ian's character gunned down a speeding zombie as they turned the corner toward the first checkpoint.

Aaron frowned as he had to go hand-to-hand with a zombie because he'd run out of ammo. Again. "I'm not sure how long we're going to still be together."

"What? No. Man, that stinks. I'm sorry. What happened?"

"I don't know. After church it was clear something was up. I offered to skip lunch, and she was happy with that, but Luca was so upset she let me stay. But I headed out as fast as I could." Luca had been bummed, but he had a book report he needed to finish —and he hadn't finished reading the book yet—so it wasn't like Aaron would have spent the afternoon playing video games with him. And still, he would have rather hung out with the two of them and helped with chores than be at home by himself shooting zombies. "Feels like the writing's on the wall. She's going to dump me, and I won't know why."

"At least you see it coming?"

"Oh yeah, that's a big help." Aaron tossed his controller on the couch as his character died. "This game is horrible."

"I don't remember it being this hard. Wanna switch to something else?"

"Yeah." Aaron pressed a button and exited to the home screen. He and Ian had a lot of the same games, so it shouldn't take too long to settle on something else.

"Do you think she'll let you hang out with Luca now and then if she ends things? You talk about him enough. It's pretty obvious you're attached."

Aaron's chest ached. "I think he might be mine."

There was a long pause. *"What?"*

Aaron squeezed his eyes shut. He hadn't meant to say that aloud. He'd been actively working on keeping from even thinking it. "Never mind."

"No way. Not in this lifetime. You can't drop a bomb like that and then expect to back away. You knew Holly before? Why haven't you said something? I didn't realize you were exes. That paints all of this in a different light."

"We're not exes. We never dated."

"But you said . . . I guess I'm not following."

Which was why Aaron had tried to back away from this conversation. He dragged a hand through his hair. Maybe it would help to talk it out with someone. Or it would make it worse. How was he supposed to know? "Do you want to come over? I have a steak in the fridge. I could grill it and throw together a salad or something."

"I like steak. I bought those frozen twice-baked potatoes the other day—I'll bring them and some fried mozzarella sticks. Also frozen. Because I'm a bachelor without a woman in my life, who doesn't do fancy food like you do, apparently. If you really want to make a salad, you can do that, too."

Aaron laughed. "That actually sounds really good. We can skip the salad."

"Deal. Probably be there in about twenty? Thirty if traffic is messed up."

"All right. I'm going to try that demo you gave me then until you get here."

"Works. Later."

Aaron watched as Ian's avatar went offline. There was no point in grilling until Ian got here. It wouldn't take anywhere near the kind of time the frozen food would. Although . . . he frowned and set his controller aside so he could jog upstairs and into the kitchen. The oven took forever to pre-heat, so he might as well get that going now. Then it'd be ready, or close to, when Ian showed up. He punched in four hundred degrees and hit Bake. If that wasn't exactly what they needed, it'd be close enough.

Satisfied that he'd done his part to speed things along, he went back to the Xbox and loaded up the demo that Ian had handed out at the last men's Bible study. It was some sort of treasure hunting puzzle combo. Not his usual choice, but it had sounded fun. And he wasn't going to turn down a free game.

He'd made it to level seven by the time the doorbell rang. Aaron paused the game and stood, stretching his arms up over his head. That had to have been more than thirty minutes.

Upstairs, Aaron checked the peep before opening the door.

"Sorry. My mom called as I was leaving, and she gets angry if I don't give her my undivided attention." Ian stepped in and thrust a grocery store bag at Aaron. "Here's the food. We could cook them now, even if we did the steak later. I could go for a snack."

"Sure." Aaron took the bag and headed into the kitchen. A glance at the clock on the stove said it had been a little over an hour. The ache in his back made more sense now. He usually tried to get up and stretch every thirty when he was gaming. His couch was comfortable, but it was old and could cause kinks if he wasn't careful. "You want to grab a sheet tray from the cabinet under the microwave?"

"Yeah, okay." Ian dug around and finally set the tray on the island. "So. Start talking."

Dang it. Aaron had been half hoping that Ian would forget the reason he came over. He sighed as he ripped open one end of the box of mozzarella sticks and dumped them onto the tray. "Okay, you know how I was in college, right?"

"Sort of? You've said a few things here and there, but I don't know details."

Of course not. He frowned and arranged the cheese in even lines. He checked the box for the time and temperature, then he looked at the potato skin box. "These need wildly different temps. Should we do the cheese first and save the skins for the steak?"

"Sure. Whatever." Ian scooted onto a stool and pointed a finger at him. "Quit stalling."

Aaron shook his head and stuck the cheese into the oven. He set the timer before returning to the island and leaning against it. "I pledged a frat my freshman year. They were all about partying, and I was on board with that. I didn't really know Jesus. My parents dragged us to church, so I knew all the right words to say, but it never hit my heart, you know? It was all about hanging out with the youth group to have fun."

Ian nodded.

"Anyway, I was at college for the whole college experience. In my mind, that was more about sex, friends, and parties than anything else. The degree was a necessary evil to keep me there."

"I knew guys like you. I *hated* guys like you."

Aaron nodded. "Not surprised. By junior year, if there wasn't a party on campus that sounded interesting, me and a couple of other guys would head down to Tech. There were always good parties there, if you knew where to look."

"Okay. I guess that's true. I didn't pay a lot of attention."

Aaron had forgotten Ian went to Tech, too. Then again, so did half of the world, it seemed. With a student body of more than thirty thousand, on average, maybe it wasn't too far off. "Right. Anyway, from a few things Holly has said, it's possible, man."

"And the boy—you really think he could be yours?"

Aaron took his phone out of his pocket and opened his photo gallery. "Look at him."

"He's cute." Ian frowned at the picture, his head tilting to the side. "I mean, I guess I can see a resemblance? I wouldn't say it was something I'd spot walking down the street."

Aaron took his phone back and swiped to the pictures he'd had his mom scan and email. "What about this one?"

Ian laughed. "Was it retro day at school? Where'd she even find pants like that?"

"That's me. At nine."

Ian's eyebrows shot up. "Oh. Wow."

"Yeah." Aaron raked his hands through his hair. "What do I do?"

"You need to find out. Don't you?"

"Yeah, but how? I can't just say, 'Oh hey, by the way, I'm pretty sure I'm your son's father.' She's already pulling away. That'd send her screaming in the other direction." The timer beeped. Aaron got pot holders out of a drawer and grabbed the tray out of the oven. He slid the cheese sticks onto the island and turned to get down some plates.

"What about DNA testing?" Ian picked up a cheese stick and bounced it back and forth between his hands. "They're hot."

"Ovens will do that." Aaron offered a weak smile and picked up a cheese stick. He broke it in half and let the stringy, melted cheese ooze in strands between the parts. A DNA test wasn't a horrible idea, but how would he even go about it? Was it something he could do behind Holly's back? Was he stupid for even asking that question? But what if he wasn't Luca's dad? Would it be better to keep it from her so she wasn't disappointed?

Would she be disappointed? Or relieved?

"I can hear your gears spinning." Ian bit into his third cheese stick, hissing out the heat before closing his mouth to chew.

"I just wish there were answers. It's all questions."

"You've been praying, right?"

Aaron nodded. Kind of. "Not about that, specifically."

"Start. I'll join you."

"Okay. Thanks."

Ian wiped his fingers on his jeans before digging out his phone. He tapped at it, then swiveled it around. "I wondered and, sure enough, a quick search reveals that there are at home paternity tests. Oral swabs that you send off, and they're a hundred bucks."

Aaron hadn't looked it up. He'd assumed the collection would be like the ancestry testing. His parents had done that and Mom had gone on for hours about how gross it was to spit enough to fill the container. Maybe cheek swabs would be easier to sneak. Somehow. "I'll think on it."

"And pray." Ian took another cheese stick.

"And pray." Hopefully God would make it obvious what Aaron should do. Even if Holly didn't want to be together—he ignored the sharp stab of hurt at the thought—if Luca was his son, Aaron was going to be in the boy's life.

10

Aaron looked up at the tap on his office door. "Come in."

"Hi." Holly peeked in. "Do you have a minute?"

"Sure." He leaned back in his chair, his stomach tightening. "What's up?"

She cleared her throat as she stepped in and shut the door behind her. She clasped her hands behind her back and hovered near the door. "I—it's about last Sunday."

He nodded. Of course, it was. She'd avoided him thoroughly yesterday, and most of today. Maybe it was good, now that it was nearly the end of the day on Tuesday, that she was ready to talk. Except, looking at her face, she didn't have positive things on her mind. "Okay?"

"Look. I don't know how to do this. I don't want you to take it the wrong way or be hurt. Or anything like that."

"Holly."

She stopped and took a deep breath. "Don't be nice right now. Please. I can't do this. I need us to take a step back. Apart. Away. There's too much to focus on right now, with the contest and Luca and just everything and as much as I love kissing you and how that makes me feel, it's not the right time."

Aaron swallowed. Words jumbled on his tongue, but he held them back. *A little help here, God? Please?* "Is it the kissing that's the problem? We could back off on that."

"No. Aaron, it's all of it. Don't you understand? It would be so easy to let you in our lives. You fit—there's no question that you fit—but that makes it worse. Luca adores you. I'm not far behind. And I don't know how to navigate heartbreak when both of us are suffering from it."

"So you're breaking up with me so you don't get hurt if things don't work out between us?" He frowned even as his heart shattered into pieces.

"Yes. No. It sounds stupid when you say it like that." She frowned.

"Then maybe you shouldn't do it." He offered a hopeful smile and started to stand.

"Please stay there. I need to do this. If you touch me—if you kiss me—I won't have the courage. We have to keep working together. And we can be friends. But that has to be it. Okay? Please understand."

He shook his head. "I don't understand though. I love you."

"Don't say that." Her hands flew up and covered her ears. "Don't make this worse."

"Holly." He stood and crossed to her, stopping when he was close enough to reach out and touch her. But he didn't. It took all the restraint he had not to, but he was going to respect her wishes. Even if it killed him. He held her gaze. "I love you. I love Luca. I don't want this to end."

She shook her head, her eyes shiny with tears. "You can't."

"But I do." His eyes burned. "I'll step back, because you say you need me to. But please, don't rip Luca completely out of my life. For him and for me. We could hang out without you, here and there. It could be a break for you."

"I . . . maybe. I don't want you to feel obligated."

Obligated? If he had his way, he'd be even more *obligated*. He considered bringing up a paternity test and rejected it just as fast. He'd get a kit and, the next time he saw Luca, talk the kid into it. Maybe if he posed it as a science experiment? He'd have to think some—it needed to be something Luca wouldn't immediately blab to Holly about. Aaron knew better than to ask the boy to keep it secret—that was what creepers did. Kids and adults should never have secrets. "I don't. I love him."

She held up a hand. "Stop. I'll think about it. Don't be mad. Please."

"I'm not." Mad wasn't on the long list of things he was feeling. Sick. Aching. Heartbroken. All of those, for sure. But not mad. "I guess I'll be praying you change your mind."

A smile flashed briefly on Holly's lips. "I did have something else—not personal."

His eyebrows lifted.

"You remember I mentioned the traffic was spiking in the middle of the night?"

"Sure. But there are people in other time zones." He shrugged. "I looked and didn't think it was anything to worry about."

"I know. You could be right. But they're getting bigger—longer. I just think we ought to do something."

"Like what?" Traffic spikes weren't his domain. They weren't even something he thought about. Ever. The only reason he even understood what she was talking about was because Holly had gone over it in great detail the first time she'd noticed it.

She shrugged.

He shook his head. How was he supposed to switch gears

like this? He couldn't focus—he looked at her and saw the woman who'd just smashed his heart to pieces. And he was supposed to care about traffic spikes on a server somewhere? "Look, I don't think it's a big deal. If you do, why don't you talk to someone in Cyber? Jessica Ward is part of the contest, right? Go see her. Maybe she'll be able to figure it out."

Holly brightened. "That's a great idea. Thanks."

"Sure." He tucked his hands in his pockets. "Is that it?"

She nodded. "I'm really sorry, Aaron."

"Me, too."

Holly opened her mouth and drew in a breath. She snapped her lips closed and shook her head. "I'll see you later."

"Yeah. See you." He turned and stalked to his window. He looked out over Tyson's Corner and ignored the snick of his office door closing. He lowered his forehead to the cool glass and closed his eyes.

Now what?

HOLLY WOUND her way through the maze of cubes on the floor of the building occupied by the cyber security division. How had her life come to this? She'd been chugging along, doing what she needed to do to provide for herself and Luca. No one had noticed her—or at least that was what it seemed like. Obviously, someone had noticed since she got chosen to participate in this bizarre contest idea of Joe Robinson, CEO, owner, and founder of Robinson Enterprises.

She should have said no.

Of course, no one said no. Not when the bait dangled in front of them was the chance to take over the day-to-day operations of a major division of the company. The chance to direct the future and, oh yeah, the salary package and perks that went along with that sort of position.

She sighed.

She hadn't seen Aaron Powell coming. And that was on her. She'd spent the last nine years hyper alert when it came to men. How had she fallen so far so fast with the man she was supposed to be working with slash competing against?

He had said he loved her.

And Luca.

So of course she'd had to end things.

Holly hadn't gone into his office planning to completely break things off. She'd been primed to suggest a break—a step back—maybe just stopping the whole church thing. It wasn't clear. But when Aaron had said he loved her? She'd known. Reverse thrusters on full.

She loved him. She'd had a few words with God last night when that realization had hit. His will was so twisty and turny and impossible to understand. It was ridiculous and unfair. And fine, she sounded like a petulant child. She was okay with that at this point.

If she hadn't broken things off, would Aaron have taken her concerns with the traffic spikes more seriously? Would he have arranged a meeting with the Cyber people? She didn't know them. She didn't know anyone. Ugh. Now she was on her own.

She double-checked the nameplate affixed to the cube wall by an opening, then cleared her throat. "Excuse me. Are you Jessica Ward?"

The woman swiveled in her desk chair and cocked her head to the side. "Sure am. Jess. How can I help?"

"I'm Holly. Holly Bell. I'm with SociaLinks?"

Jess nodded. "Sure. You're part of the contest."

"Yeah. But this isn't about that. I was talking to Aaron, and he kind of blew me off, but he said if I was really concerned to talk to someone in Cyber. So here I am." Maybe she shouldn't have brought up Aaron, but it wasn't like she was here right out of the gate. Jess seemed busy. Holly felt like she was intruding. And that was making her run off at the mouth.

"Here you are. Do you want to sit?" Jess pointed to her guest chair.

"Oh. Sure. Thanks." Holly came into Jess's cube and sat. "Um. I don't know if you know how we're set up. Or maybe it doesn't matter. But we use cloud servers for all the hosting. So the app connects up that way."

"Right. That's pretty common these days. Standard, even. Very few people want to bother with in-house server farms when the big warehouses are more affordable and have experts on-site. Are you having trouble with the server farm? That's not really what we do, but I can try to take a look. That said, there's probably tech support if there's a physical issue that needs to be investigated."

"No. At least I don't think so." Holly clenched and unclenched her hands. Jess wasn't the friendliest woman, was she? Or maybe it was just that Holly wasn't doing this right. Nerves jumping in her belly were distracting, and they'd kicked off the "you're not good enough" tape that ran in her brain. "Sorry, I'm really bungling this. I think our servers are under attack."

"Oh? Now that *is* something we do." Jess grinned. "Tell me what makes you think that."

Holly breathed out a relieved sigh. Maybe this *wasn't* going to be a huge waste of everyone's time. "Okay. Part of what I do every morning is a quick traffic check. It's good data for all our stats—and those stats feed feature rollout and marketing and just everything."

"Sure. Stats make the world go round."

"Seems like it, doesn't it?" Holly offered a shy smile. "Anyway, Aaron thinks I'm overreacting, but there's been a big spike two days running. Two a.m. And that's way outside our usual traffic patterns, even factoring in international use. And it's not recent. The big one, yeah, two days, but there have been smaller ones that were still outside the realm of normal, I thought at least, for maybe a month? I dug into the IP addresses a little and they just seem hinky."

"Hinky." Jess bit her lip.

Holly's cheeks heated. "Sorry. I have a weird vocabulary. Everyone says so."

"Don't worry about it. It's a cool word. I'm happy to look into it."

"Oh. Thank you. I went ahead and created an account for you with admin access because I was hoping I could convince you to take a look." Holly handed Jess a sheet of paper with the details she'd need. "Could you change the password when you get in, though? I don't like knowing a default is out there, even when it's something I made up."

"Absolutely. It might take me a little time. I can come find you when I know something." Jess took the paper and set it beside her mouse.

"Oh. Right. Ha." Holly stood, her hands flitting at her sides. In some ways, that had been easier than she expected. In other ways, she couldn't stop thinking about how dismissive Aaron had been about the whole thing. What if this was all for nothing? Was she wasting everyone's time? "I appreciate this. I can figure out a charge code if you need me to. I don't know how stuff like this—you helping me when we're not in the same division—is going to work when the contest ends. Will we be more separate companies?"

Jess shrugged. "I'm not sure. But since Joe's not really spinning us all off on our own, more just setting a stronger management structure so he doesn't have to stay so hands-on with everything, I imagine this will still be able to happen. There'll still be interdivisional overhead. I use those codes periodically. I'll just find the one for Social and use it, if that's all right?"

"It should be. I'll double-check and let you know if it isn't." How had she not known there were interdivisional charge codes? That definitely made it easier. And of course Joe had something like this in place already. Maybe Holly wasn't as cut out for this promotion as she wanted to believe she was.

"That works." Jess smiled. "It might be tomorrow. I may need to see the spike in progress to trace and track more accurately."

"Do what you need to do. And if you come back and need to tell me it's nothing and I'm paranoid, that's okay."

Jess chuckled. "Good to know."

"Okay. Well, bye." Holly waved and slipped out of Jess's cubicle. She hurried down to the aisle, turned the corner, then sagged against the wall. She was a smart, capable woman. Why was it so hard to step out from behind her computer monitor? She pushed off the wall and headed back to the elevators. She'd survived. That was the key. And Jess was going to look into things, which was also key.

If it was nothing, fine, she'd apologize for wasting everyone's time. Something in her gut said it wasn't nothing. At this point, all she could do was wait and see.

Should she let Aaron know Jess was looking into it?

No.

He'd brushed her off. He didn't want to have any more interaction with her than absolutely necessary right now. At least the March assignment was a self-evaluation. They'd already written up the combined eval of how they worked as a team. So now it was up to her to do her own part and email it to Aaron for him to comment on. And he'd do the same.

But they didn't need to meet to do it. And right now, that was a blessing.

Holly made her way back to her cube, pulled up her task list for the day, and got to work. The busier she kept, the less thinking she'd do about Aaron. The less she thought about Aaron, the sooner her broken heart would heal.

11

"Why can't we have dinner with Mr. Aaron like we usually do?" Luca crossed his arms and scowled at Holly across the kitchen table.

She sighed. She'd been avoiding this conversation all week, but it looked like the time had come. Holly tapped the wooden spoon against the side of the pot of soup she was making for supper, turned the heat down to low, and moved to the table. She sat across from him and waited until he looked up. "Aaron and I aren't seeing each other anymore."

Luca's scowl deepened, but he didn't speak.

Please God, I need the right words. She took a deep breath and tried to pick her way through the minefield. "You remember I told you about the contest at work. The one for the big promotion?"

He nodded.

"Well Mr. Aaron and I are working together on that. And sort of competing. It's a little complicated. But that doesn't matter. The point is, we got thrown together into this stressful situation and for a little while, it felt like maybe God was calling us to more than friendship. But that doesn't look like it's going to be the case." It was a horrible explanation, but it was the best she could do right now. She couldn't explain why to Luca when she didn't understand it herself. Her heart was still breaking a little more every day that she had to go without Aaron. How had she come to rely on him so fully so fast?

"But he did the donuts with me. I thought that meant he liked me."

"Oh, honey, he does. He loves you. He said that." He'd said he loved her, too. Holly's eyes burned. She looked down at her hands and battled back the tears. She'd never be able to explain them to Luca.

"Just not enough to keep hanging out with me."

"No. He wants that, too. He said so." Holly closed her eyes. What was she supposed to do? "Do you want me to see if he'd like to come over and play video games tomorrow afternoon? Or maybe you could go to his house."

Luca brightened.

It wasn't what she wanted. At all. But maybe it was best. Luca deserved to have an adult male in his life. He didn't have a father. Now that her parents had moved, he didn't really have a grandfather, either. Not like her dad had done a bang-up job to begin with, but he'd been better than nothing. So. Aaron. He'd said he wanted that. She'd see if he'd been telling the truth. "I'll text him after dinner."

"Okay." He studied her, his gaze intense. "Are you okay, Mom? You look sad."

She smiled and stood before leaning across the table to ruffle his hair. "I'll be fine. I'm a little tired."

"Is that why we're having soup and grilled cheese?"

She laughed. "Part of it, yes. Plus, I know a little boy who likes it and I wanted something I didn't have to fight to get him to eat."

"Mo-om."

"What?" She winked at him over her shoulder. "Did you choose the movie for tonight yet?"

"Dunno. Do you have one you want to watch?"

Holly frowned as she flipped over a grilled cheese. Luca had been adamant that they watch the Marvel movies with Aaron. Aaron. Now that he was gone, had Luca lost his interest? Or was he trying to save them in case Aaron came back around? "What's next in the order?"

"Oh. I know you don't want to watch superheroes, Mom. We can pick something else."

Holly dished up supper and took it over to the table. She sat down and reached for Luca's hand. He bowed his head. Then looked back up when she didn't start praying immediately.

"I'm interested in what you want to watch. You're my priority. I love you. You know that, right?" Holly squeezed his hand.

"Yeah, I know." He smiled. "Love you, too."

She waited, but he didn't say more. Holly squeezed his hand and bowed her head. Aloud, she offered a quick prayer for the food. In her heart, she begged God to show her what to do. Losing Aaron had been hard enough—necessary, she stood by that—but hard. She didn't want to lose even a smidgen of Luca.

They ate, and Holly worked to keep a conversation going. Luca didn't want to talk about school, beyond saying it was boring. She tried his friends, his homework, what he was learning, anything she could think of. If she was lucky, he gave her more than one word as an answer.

She wasn't lucky very often.

Finally, the plates were clean. "Why don't you run upstairs and get ready for bed. Jammies, find all the stuffed animals you want to sleep with, that kind of thing. Then come back down and we'll watch a movie and eat popcorn."

"I don't need popcorn. I'm stuffed." Luca scooted his chair back and trudged out of the kitchen.

Holly stared after him before burying her face in her hands. This was why she hadn't dated since Luca was born. She'd *known* it was going to blow up in her face, and she'd done it anyway. Why?

Because she was a glutton for punishment, apparently.

Speaking of which . . . she dragged her phone out of her pocket and opened a text message. Might as well deal with tomorrow and get it done.

HI. IT'S HOLLY. LUCA WAS HOPING YOU MIGHT BE INTERESTED IN SOME XBOX TIME TOMORROW. IT'S OKAY IF YOU AREN'T. EITHER WAY, JUST LET ME KNOW?

There. She hit Send and set the phone on the table. She collected the dishes and carried them to the sink where she rinsed them before loading them into the dishwasher. Technically, it was Luca's job tonight, but the thought of asking him to do it left a sour taste in her mouth. It was easier to do it herself.

Tonight, she needed easy.

Her phone buzzed.

She turned and looked at it from across the room. Her stomach was shaky and everything tasted of metal. What if he said no? She'd tell Luca that Aaron was busy. That was all. And then she'd make time in her schedule to figure out exactly what Aaron thought it meant when he told someone he loved them.

Of course, she'd thrown that love back in his face and walked away, so that might influence future behavior.

Ugh! She didn't even know what he'd texted and she was making up a worst-case scenario.

Holly took a deep breath and marched to the table. She picked up her phone and tapped the screen.

LOVE TO. WHAT TIME CAN I PICK HIM UP?

She blew out her breath. Okay. Good. This was good. She thought through their schedule. They didn't have anything pressing—at least not if Luca had been honest about his weekend homework schedule. She tapped back a reply.

Let's say 1? That way you don't have to feed him. Have him home by 4:30?

Holly bit her lip before hitting Send. She didn't want Luca to be a strain on Aaron's Saturday. And that was plenty of video game time, even if she factored in the drive to Aaron's house. It was enough. She sent the message.

Aaron responded almost immediately.

I never mind feeding him, but that's fine. Tell him I'm looking forward to it.

Was this the right thing? She wasn't worried about Luca's safety—she trusted Aaron—but how would this work if they weren't a couple? Aaron didn't have any reason to want to be involved with Luca long term. So what? Was he eventually going to change his mind and leave Luca even worse off?

Her fingers hovered over the phone. Finally, she tapped out one more reply.

If you decide down the road you don't want to be part of Luca's life anymore, would you tell me first so I can try to make it easier for him?

I'm not going to do that.

You don't know for sure. Just . . . let me know. okay?

Holly sighed and pinched the bridge of her nose.

"I'm ready!" Luca slid into the kitchen in his socks and Hulk pajamas.

"Okay, Hulk, let's go." Holly pushed her thoughts of Aaron and her worry over what to do out of her mind. "You're sure you don't want popcorn?"

He shrugged.

"Does knowing that Mr. Aaron is going to pick you up for some video games tomorrow afternoon change anything?"

"He is?" Luca's whole being brightened. He threw his arms around Holly and squeezed tight. "You're the best mom."

Holly kissed the top of his head. "I love you, buddy."

"Can we watch a cartoon?"

"Sure. Old or new?"

Luca considered the options—out loud—as he led the way downstairs. Holly rubbed the spot over her heart, but it did nothing to ease the ache.

AARON STOPPED outside the door to the condo where his men's Bible study met and pulled out his phone. He'd been checking email with Pavlovian consistency every time it dinged to let him know something new had arrived. He'd done the paternity test on Luca two Saturdays ago when he'd had him over for Xbox time.

He hadn't been sure about it. He *still* wasn't sure about it, if he was honest with himself, because it seemed wrong to have gone behind Holly's back to find out. But if he'd asked, would she have allowed it?

He'd been on edge the whole week between, waiting for her to storm into his office and demand answers. Aaron hadn't said anything about the test being a secret. He'd said it was a fun science experiment. Luca hadn't asked questions. If Aaron was honest, some small part of him had hoped Luca would spill the beans and force the confrontation. Then he wouldn't have to be the one seeking her out. If he was Luca's dad.

The big if.

But Aaron knew.

It was too much for him not to be certain. Between her going to Tech and the big party with excessive drinking and, more than likely, some kind of chemical assistance even if she hadn't known about it, then throw in the fact that Luca was the spitting image of Aaron as a child? There was no way it was all coincidence.

No way.

He looked at his email inbox and froze. There were the results. His stomach knotted into a hard, hot ball. He'd been drawn in by the two-day result promise, and he hadn't factored in that they meant business days, or that he'd had to mail the swabs there in the first place. Two days for results, but a full week plus a couple of days from the time of the test.

And now he couldn't bring himself to open the email and see.

The condo door opened, and Christopher leaned against the jamb. "Hey, man. You coming in?"

Aaron bit his lip. He glanced at the email again and clicked the power button of his phone. It could wait another few hours. "Yeah. Sorry. Distracted."

Christopher chuckled. "It happens. Ian's already here, so we can start whenever."

"No Ryan?" Aaron shot Christopher a curious look as he waved to Ian and took a seat on the far end of the sofa. It was already weird enough that they'd taken a break from having dinner together first, but now Ryan was bailing?

"He's in Colorado, visiting his folks." Ian shrugged. "It was news to me, too."

Interesting. "Why?"

Christopher sighed and scrubbed hands over his face. "Turns out he's been dating Jess. And they were hiding it from me, because I guess they figured I'd be ticked."

"Were you?" Aaron cocked his head to the side.

"Well, yeah. But come on, he's been my best friend forever. I think my need for a little adjusting time should be allowed."

Ian snorted. "Was that all you needed?"

"Geez. Am I that horrible?" Christopher frowned at both of them. "Fine. No. I lost it, okay? Some of that was because their timing was horrible and Stephanie and I were in limbo, and you know what? I still think I should get some grace here. I came around and apologized to both of them."

"But? I mean, Ryan deserted the field. That suggests things are not well between him and Jess."

"Ian has a point. A good one." Aaron fist bumped Ian. "So?"

"She dumped him. And it's my fault. And now? When I look at the situation with them? They really are perfect for each other. Just like one of them said: who better to love and cherish my sister than my oldest, dearest friend?"

"Ouch." Aaron winced. Those were some wise, and yet still cutting, words. "Which one said that?"

"I don't remember. It wasn't my finest moment. I'm trying to blot it out of my brain." Christopher sighed. "I guess I'm just praying that they'll manage to work it out despite my interference."

Ian nodded and tapped on his phone. "I'll do the same. Things okay now with you and Steph?"

Christopher beamed. "They are. I know it's soon, but I've already started looking at engagement rings."

"Dude. No. You just got back together." Aaron shook his head even as a warning bell rang in the back of his head. It was all well and good to warn his friend, but if he thought Holly would say yes, he'd be on his knee in front of her in a heartbeat.

"I know. I get that. I'll wait a little bit, but not super long. I love her. She loves me. And I can't escape the certainty here," he banged his chest, "that she's the woman God has for me."

"Wow. Good for you, man." Ian tapped at his phone some more. "I'll pray about that, too."

"Yeah. I can do that, too." Aaron opened his phone. The email program was still open and the results from the test called to him. He looked at the two men he considered brothers. He cleared his throat. "Since we're on the topic of prayer requests, I have an email that I need to open. Maybe you guys could pray with me first?"

Christopher's eyebrows lifted but he nodded. "Of course. You want to fill us in now, or later?"

Aaron didn't want to fill them in at all. But that was cowardice talking. Besides, Ian already knew the details.

"Is this what I think it is?" Ian's eyes were wide.

Aaron nodded.

"Oh, wow. I see how it is." Christopher's voice held only humor, but he tried for a hurt facial expression. And failed miserably.

"Yeah, yeah. I guess it makes sense to tell the story first." Aaron blew out a breath and sketched the details of his short-lived relationship with Holly and his suspicions about Luca. "So when I was at CVS and saw I could buy a test kit for thirty bucks right there plus like a hundred more to cover the processing? I took it as a sign. Then when she texted later that night to ask about hanging with Luca the next day, I saw confirmation again. So we did the swabs—he thought it was a hilariously weird science experiment—and I sent them off."

"And now you have the results in your email?" Ian pointed at Aaron's phone.

Aaron nodded and his stomach clutched. Maybe it was a good thing they weren't eating together right now. He would have surely lost his dinner if it was recent. He swallowed. "I'm scared to open it."

"What are you going to do if he's your son?" Christopher asked.

Almost at the same time, Ian asked, "What will you do if he's not your son?"

Aaron laughed. "Those are the two questions that keep

circling in my brain. The answer is the same to both of them: I don't know."

Christopher motioned for Aaron's phone. "Here. Give it to me. I'll read them."

Should he? No. He could do this. "Thanks. I got it. Just pray, okay?"

Aaron took a deep breath and tapped the email. He scanned the blah-de-blah lawyer speak about how these weren't admissible in court. He skimmed past columns of numbers with different colored circles, to the notes underneath. Not excluded. Probability of paternity 99.99999%.

His breath came out in a whoosh. "He's mine."

"How do you feel?" Ian gestured for the phone.

Numb, Aaron handed it to him and closed his eyes. How *did* he feel? Emotions jumbled around inside him like balls in a Bingo machine. But no one was pressing a button to make one of them pop out. "I don't know."

"That seems reasonable." Christopher had the phone now and shook his head, a slight smile on his face. "Congratulations, Dad."

"Dad." The enormity of the situation pressed on him from all sides. "Oh, boy."

"You have to tell her." Christopher handed the phone back. "You know that, right? You owe Holly and Luca that much. There's child support to think of, at a minimum."

Aaron nodded. He'd do the right thing. Absolutely. But would she let him back into their lives? "I want so much more than that."

"We should pray." Ian scooted forward to the edge of his seat and made eye contact with each of them before bowing his head.

Aaron closed his eyes and tried to quiet his thoughts. That was an exercise in futility. Luca was his son! He'd missed out on nine years already. Holly hadn't known—he believed that without question. And she'd done an amazing job. But now? He wanted to help.

He wanted to be part of Luca's life.

He wanted to be part of Holly's life, too.

It was good that God was a God of miracles . . . it seemed like Aaron was going to need one.

12

Aaron made it through Tuesday. Barely. How was he supposed to bring this up to Holly? More to the point, what was the likelihood she'd ever speak to him again after he did?

It didn't matter. It wouldn't. He was going to do right by his son.

His *son*.

Aaron closed his eyes and the image of Luca appeared. A wife and family hadn't really been on his radar. Oh, sure, he dated here and there, but the memory of how empty and hopeless it was to chase that connection kept him from the apps and online dating sites. Now? It was like someone had unlocked the treasure chest that held all his hopes and dreams for the future.

A tapping at the door was followed by Holly peeking in. "You said you needed to see me?"

"Yeah. Thanks. Have a seat." Aaron gestured to the smaller round table and stood. Anything he could do to make this friendlier was a good thing. He picked up the folder that held a printout of the paternity test results. His hands were slick with sweat.

"What's going on?" Holly frowned as she pulled out a chair.

"I feel like I want to start this conversation out with please don't be mad, but if you're anything like my mom, that just makes you mad before we even start talking."

Holly's eyebrows lifted. "That's how any sane person responds to those words. What am I supposed to not be mad about?"

He took in her stiff back and crossed arms and sighed. He should have kept that to himself. He'd thought it might lighten the mood. "Do you remember when we bumped into each other at the grocery store the first time?"

"Yeah?"

"And I met Luca—although you didn't introduce him. He just called you Mom. And I was surprised, because it's not like we were complete strangers, and I had no idea you had a child."

"I just don't see the point in bringing my personal life into the office." She huffed out a breath. "Where are you going with this, Aaron? If you don't get to the point soon, I'm going to leave. We're not together anymore—and it's just as hard for me as it probably is for you—but that doesn't make it the wrong decision."

Aaron flinched. "I disagree, but that wasn't my point."

She closed her eyes for a moment and breathed in deeply. When her eyes opened, she nodded. "Sorry. What was your point?"

"Luca. I love him. I love you."

"Aaron."

"No, I know. Sorry. When we first met outside of work— before I loved him, and you—I was surprised when I saw him, because he's the spitting image of me at nine."

Holly's frown deepened and her head started to shake. "I went to Tech. You went to JMU."

"I was at Tech all the time, though. It's only a couple hours away. And the parties were usually better." He kept his gaze on her face as it paled.

"But—"

"What were the chances, right? I know. So I pushed it out of my head as long as I could, but it was never very far away. So last weekend, when he came to play Xbox, I told him we were doing a science experiment." Aaron slid the folder over to her.

Holly put her hands on top of the folder and stared at him with wide, terrified eyes. Her voice was a croaking whisper. "What did you do?"

"I had to know. Especially since you were so adamant that you didn't want me in your life anymore. He's my son, Holly."

"No." Her head was shaking faster and faster. Tears slipped down her face. "No. You can't be. I don't know who he is. I hardly remember any of it. You don't remember, either!"

"There's a lot about my weekends in college that I don't remember. I'm not proud of it—but God used it to get my attention. He's forgiven me. Redeemed me. And I'm sorry, Holly. So sorry that I took advantage of you."

"I don't—you can't—" She blinked furiously and looked away.

Aaron pressed his lips together. What was he supposed to do? He tried to pray but only managed "Help" over and over.

When Holly looked back at him, her expression was stony. "You're not taking him away from me."

"No. I don't want that. I'm not trying to take him away. I want to help."

"I don't need your help." Holly stood so fast the chair clattered to the floor. "I'm doing fine on my own. I'm a good mother. Luca doesn't want for anything."

"But I could still—"

"No!" She clamped her mouth shut and breathed in through

her nose before continuing more quietly, "No. We're fine. We don't need you."

"But I can—"

Holly held up a hand. "Stop. The answer is no. I don't care what you were going to say. It's just no."

Aaron watched as she snatched up the folder and fled from his office. He rubbed his aching chest and sighed. That could have gone better.

It was hard to imagine how it could have gone worse.

Now what, Lord?

He sat there for several minutes going over the conversation. Was there a better way to have done it? What was the protocol for letting a woman know you were the father of her child?

Aaron scrubbed a hand over his face and stood. He'd go home and do some more work there. Or maybe put on a movie and veg. He wasn't sure what he'd actually be able to accomplish if he tried to be productive.

He packed up his laptop and some files, just in case, and headed out with an absentminded wave to the admin. She tried to catch his eye and engage him in conversation, but he wasn't interested. Not today.

Thankfully, he didn't run into anyone he needed to talk to on the elevator ride down to the garage. He could handle the brief smile of acknowledgment as long as there wasn't also chit chat needed. Right now, small talk wasn't going to happen.

By the time he fought his way through the rush hour traffic to his townhouse, he was exhausted. He dumped his laptop by the door, kicked off his shoes, checked the deadbolt, and headed upstairs. A list of things he ought to do ran through his mind, but . . . they'd all be there tomorrow.

Right now? He was going to take a long, blisteringly hot shower. Then he was going to bed.

Maybe things would look brighter in the morning.

"Come on, Luca, we need to go." Holly checked the time again and tapped her foot. The car was loaded with their bags, and her parents were expecting them to arrive by lunch, which in her parents' bizarre world meant no later than eleven a.m. It was a three-hour drive. Minimum.

"I don't understand why we hafta go today. I thought you said we weren't doing anything for spring break. I've been playing with Jordan—we have a tournament going and everything. I don't even want to go to the stupid beach." Luca stomped across the foyer dragging an overstuffed pillowcase behind him. "It's not like Grandma and Grandpa live on a cool beach. It's the inlet. And Grandpa's gonna make me go flounder gigging and then we hafta eat it, too."

"They love having us, and we had a change of plans." Holly tried to keep a rein on her temper. She didn't need to take her confusion and lack of sleep out on Luca. She forced a smile. "We're going to have fun. We can go see the battleship at the museum and do the spy mission."

"I guess." Luca sighed heavily and trudged down the stairs in front of the house. "I guess that means I don't get to see Mr. Aaron on Saturday either. That's two weeks in a row."

"I know, baby." How could her heart keep breaking more each day, and with every comment from her son? And from Aaron. And knowing he was Luca's father? She should be angry —for all of it. He slept with her when she was drunk—but then, so was he. He hadn't left any information to help her get in touch with him. But then, it wasn't as if they'd gone on a date. There was no expectation of that at those sorts of parties—it was why she didn't usually go to them. Why she'd dragged her feet when her so-called friends had nagged her into going. The girls who went to those parties were usually all on birth control. And if it failed, they were the kinds of girls who didn't have an issue having an abortion to "fix the problem." She sighed.

It would be easier to be angry, but really, she was just heart-broken all over again.

It was why she wanted to go home. Even if she'd never lived in the house at the shore where her parents lived, her mom and dad were there, and that made it home. And maybe, just maybe, they'd have some suggestions for what she needed to do. Because so far, at least as Holly was able to hear, God wasn't talking.

The drive gave her too much time to think. Luca had his head buried in his tablet. She probably ought to make him do something else—read a book or stare out the window or talk to her—but she couldn't.

"Are we there yet?"

Holly managed a chuckle at Luca's question. "Look out the window, what do you see?"

Luca let out a groan. "Houses."

"So are we off the Interstate?"

"Yes." Luca started kicking the passenger seat in front of him. "So we're almost there?"

"We're almost there. Maybe five minutes. Ten if we hit traffic lights." Holly braked as the light ahead turned yellow. So, probably closer to that ten. She was anxious to get out of the car, too.

At last, she turned at the guard shack to her parents' neighborhood and punched the code into the keypad. The arm went up slowly. *Come on, come on.* Finally. Holly drove through and turned down the street toward her parents'.

"There it is! Why is Grandma outside waiting?"

Holly's gaze flicked to the dashboard. They weren't late. "I'm not sure. Why don't we ask her?"

She turned into the driveway and shifted into park. Holly pushed open the door and stepped out. "Hi, Mom."

"You made it. I was starting to worry." Mom rushed over and wrapped Holly in her arms.

Holly laughed and squeezed her mom back. "What do you mean? We're right on time for lunch."

"I know, I know, but we weren't expecting you, and then you decided to come, and I started to worry that something was wrong. Are you sick? Is it Luca?"

Luca climbed out of the car and walked over. "Hi, Grandma."

"Hi, Luca. Oh my, you've grown." Mom squeezed Luca and kissed the top of his head. "Why don't you run around to the back? Grandpa's at the end of the dock looking for flounder."

Luca shot his mom a look as his shoulders fell. "I told you."

"What's he mean?"

Holly watched as Luca trudged around the house and sighed. "He doesn't like flounder. Gigging it or eating it."

Mom waved her hands. "He needs to toughen up a little and get interested in masculine things. This is what comes of your not knowing who his father is. And you're not exactly doing anything about bringing someone else home to be a father figure."

"You know what? Maybe this was a bad idea. We'll stay for lunch and then maybe we'll find another way to spend our spring break."

"Oh, don't be like that. What did I say that wasn't true?" Mom jerked her head toward the house. "Come inside and we'll start on lunch."

It wasn't necessarily that her mom's words weren't true. They just weren't kind. Or supportive. Because Holly was simply a huge disappointment to her parents. Ever since that party—that one defining moment in her life—she'd gone from being her parents' adored daughter to the one who'd let them down. Twice.

She'd let them down first by getting pregnant. Then again when she refused to place Luca for adoption.

There had been reasons—including the fact that she'd thought her boyfriend was the father and he was going to stand by her and do the right thing. But the moment the paternity test came back negative, he'd been gone. He wasn't going to raise another man's child.

Holly's eyes burned and she battled back the tears. She was done crying over all of this. And maybe coming to her parents' had been the wrong choice at the end of the day.

She followed her mom into the garage that took up the ground-floor level, then up the stairs to the main floor. Mom was in the kitchen staring at the fridge.

"Oh, there you are." Mom turned and smiled. "What about grilled cheese?"

"That sounds good. Why don't you let me make it?" Holly moved to the sink and washed her hands.

"Would you? That's lovely." Mom sat at the kitchen table with a sigh. "So, what made you decide to come down after all? Last you said, you couldn't take the time off right now."

Holly grabbed the loaf of bread and opened it. She pulled out slices of bread while she thought about how to respond. After Mom's initial outburst, Holly wasn't sure about talking the whole thing through. But what were her other options?

"I've been seeing someone. I think I mentioned Aaron." She looked up.

Mom nodded. "But then you stopped talking about him. Did you break up with him?"

"Sort of." Could it be completely off when Aaron had to be part of their lives forever going forward? She might have stormed out of his office yesterday, but that had been shock more than anything. Luca deserved his dad. Especially when that dad was a man like Aaron. "Turns out, he's Luca's dad."

"He's . . . oh. That changes things, I guess."

Holly swallowed. There was no response to that. Certainly not a necessary one. She continued buttering bread.

"Will you marry him?"

Holly pressed her lips together. "I don't think we're at that point yet."

"But you're working toward it?"

Were they? Should they? Her heart yearned for him, but how was she supposed to trust it? "I don't know."

"Does Luca know?"

"No. And he can't. Not yet." Holly held her mother's gaze until she nodded slowly. Good. At least she'd gotten that agreement. Luca would have to know, obviously, but that was something Holly and Aaron could tell him together.

Together. She frowned and slapped cheese on the slices of bread she'd arranged on the griddle that was inset in her mom's stovetop, then covered them. She checked the heat and adjusted it slightly. "What am I supposed to do?"

"What does Aaron say?"

Holly tapped the spatula against the counter. "I might have stormed off when I found out."

"Oh, Holly." Mom shook her head. "You need to talk to this man and figure things out with him. You're parents. Work together."

"That's the thing, Mom, we work together. What if we break up? What if—"

"What if the sky falls on your head? Honestly, Holly, we didn't raise you to worry like this. Think it through, make a plan, execute it, and adapt as necessary."

"What about God's will?"

"What about it?"

"Shouldn't I be seeking it? I mean, what if I ended up at that party because I was outside of God's will and so then Luca is some kind of divine punishment?" Holly pried up the corner of one of the sandwiches. Not quite ready to flip.

"Oh, honey. It's good—so good that you want to be in God's will. But, you can't let yourself get paralyzed while you're seeking it. Ultimately, what is God's will? He wants us to know Him and grow in our relationship with Him. That's God's will. And He's going to use the things in our life to accomplish that. The choices we make can take us out of God's best plan, absolutely. I'm not saying it was God's will for you to get drunk and pregnant—but He knew you would. And so He had a plan to use it to bring you back to Him. So if you love this man—Aaron—and loving him, marrying him, will bring you closer to God? Will help improve your relationship with God? Then it's okay if you do that. The party, Luca—God's used all of this to bring you closer to Him. Maybe not the way I would have chosen or Dad would have wanted, but we're proud of you. I think maybe you forget that sometimes."

Was that all there was to it? It certainly simplified the confusion in her mind about free will versus God's plan—or maybe it helped set it aside when it was something she'd probably never fully understand this side of heaven. Because at the end of the day, Mom was right. The most important thing was that she was moving closer to God every day and making the choices and decisions that would help her do that. She started flipping sandwiches.

"Do you love him?"

Holly glanced up at her mom then back at the food. Did she? She ached for him, but was that love, or was it just because it had been so long since she'd had any sort of feelings for someone?

"You're taking too long. Over-thinking again." Mom shook her head as she stood and moved to a cabinet. She started taking down plates. "Just blurt out your answer. Do you love Aaron?"

"Yes." Holly closed her eyes. "But I don't know if that's smart or not."

Mom patted Holly's shoulder and reached across to turn off the griddle. "You'll figure it out. Why don't you tell me about him?"

Holly looked past her mom and through the bay window to the dock below. She could see Luca sitting on the edge, his feet dangling over the side, talking animatedly with her father, who sat beside him. They didn't look like they'd be moving anytime soon unless they were called. "We should eat first, before the cheese stops being melted."

"Fine. You can tell me about him later. Just one thing. Does he make you feel safe?"

"Yes." That was easy. With Aaron, she'd always felt safe. Protected. Worthwhile.

Cherished.

He said he loved Luca and he loved her.

As risky as it seemed, maybe it was time to believe him.

13

Holly lingered away from the dispersing crowd. The Easter service had ended, as it did every year, with a trip out to the ten-foot-tall cross that the pastor and youth pastor set up every Good Friday on the front of the church property. After the Easter service, one family group at a time, people moved forward to put fresh flowers on the cross, a beautiful symbol of Christ's resurrection for the neighborhood to enjoy.

It was a beautiful reminder for Holly, too, that God could make beauty out of everything. Even the darkest times.

She glanced down at Luca and slipped her arm around his shoulders. He was proof of God's goodness and ability to redeem the worst things. How did she ever let herself forget that? Because life got busy and the small trials of the day took her eyes easily off the big picture. It probably happened to everyone.

"Can I go play?" Luca pointed to the swing set and climbing structure that stood over by the children's building.

Several of his friends were already hollering as they zoomed around while their parents talked in little groups. "Yeah, that's fine. Stay at the playground."

"Thanks!" He grinned up at her before dashing off.

Holly opened her mouth to remind him to stay clean, but stopped herself. He was going to have more fun if he wasn't worried about getting his khakis dirty. And they'd wash. It wasn't as if he was in a suit and tie.

She looked back at the cross and prayed for wisdom.

"I've never seen this before."

Holly jolted. She knew it was Aaron before she turned. She heard his voice in her dreams. "I hadn't before we came to Cornerstone, either, but I like it."

"It reminds me of Aslan."

Her eyebrows lifted. A flowered cross reminded him of a lion in a children's book?

He must have seen her confusion because he chuckled, hands stuffed in the pockets of his dress pants. "When he comes back to life, when the stone table breaks, and he's springing around the meadow and everywhere he lands, flowers grow?"

Holly smiled. "I'd forgotten that part. Maybe it's time to re-read the Narnia books. Luca was a lot younger when I read them to him. He'd probably enjoy them even more now."

Aaron nodded. "I always loved them. Still do, in fact."

Holly waited. Maybe it made her a chicken, but she wasn't sure how to start this conversation. Except Aaron didn't seem to be in a hurry to talk, either. Were they simply going to stand outside in awkward silence for the rest of the afternoon? "Why are you here, Aaron?"

His laugh held no mirth. "I wanted to see you. And Luca."

"I'm sorry. That came out all wrong." Holly looked over at the playground and searched the throng of kids for Luca. She finally spotted him hiding under one of the platforms. She turned her gaze back to Aaron and warmed. He was like the sun drawing the attention of a budding flower. "I was going to call you this evening and see if we could have lunch tomorrow."

"We can do that."

"Or maybe we could have lunch today?" To her ears, the question sounded pathetically hopeful. Vulnerable, despite her having aimed at casual.

"I'd like that better. Why?" He took a step closer, but kept his hands in his pockets.

She wanted to dodge the question. More than anything in the world, she would like to find a way to keep from risking her heart. But Mom and Dad both had reminded her—more than once—that bravery required honesty, and honesty meant allowing for potential rejection. "Because I love you. And I'm sorry—for running, for being angry, for shutting you out—all of it. And if nothing else, because Luca deserves to know that his dad is an amazing, godly man."

"I'm trying to be. I don't think I'm completely there yet."

Holly laughed. "None of us are."

His lips curved slightly and he took another step closer, so their toes almost touched. "I'm sorry, too. For going behind your back instead of addressing my questions head on, for being pushy, and for having not been the kind of man God wanted me to be in college. I injured you then, and I can only pray that someday you'll forgive me."

"I already have. I did that before I knew you. I had to, for me." Her eyes burned and a single hot tear slid down her cheek. "But now, knowing the truth and knowing you? It's easier to let it go. To see how God has used it, even back then, for my good."

Aaron reached up and gently wiped the tear off her cheek. He lowered his forehead to hers and held her gaze. "Do you think you could say the first thing again?"

Holly thought back, then grinned. "I love you."

His eyes closed. "I've spent the last several days wondering if I'd ever have the chance to hear you say that."

"We went to the beach. My parents live there. It's not my

favorite spot—or Luca's—but I can always find time to think when I'm there. And to pray. And maybe I listen for God better there, I don't know. I did email you to let you know where we were."

He laughed. "You did. You also said not to email, text, call, or send smoke signals."

"Maybe that was a little extreme."

"Just a little. I doubt very much you would have seen any smoke signals I sent anyway."

Holly shifted closer. She wrapped her arms around his waist and rested her head on his shoulder. His arms came around her, holding her close. "Aaron?"

"Yes?"

"You said before that you loved me. Will you say it again?" She tipped her head so she could meet his gaze.

Aaron's smile melted everything in her. "I love you."

"And Luca?"

"And Luca." He tilted his head to the side. "You know I'm not going to take him from you, don't you? I just want to be in his life."

Holly took a deep breath and glanced over toward the playground to check on her son. Now he was zooming around the structure, chased by his best friend, who was letting out war whoops with glee. She turned her attention back to Aaron. "About that?"

His eyebrows lifted and his expression flattened.

Holly raised a hand and cupped his cheek. "I was hoping you'd be willing to take us both on."

A tiny line formed between Aaron's eyebrows. "What do you—"

"Marry me. Us. Be Luca's dad for real." Her heart pounded in her chest. Could he hear it? Was it too much, too soon?

Aaron's mouth crushed into hers. This wasn't a gentle, searching kiss, but one full of passion and promise and relief.

He eased back, his eyes shining with unshed tears. "Okay. Do I get a ring?"

Holly's laugh might have bordered on hysterical, but that was only because it suddenly felt as if gravity had disappeared and she was weightless. Floating. She swiped at the tears that trickled down her cheeks. "I'll see what I can do. I was kind of hoping you might get me one, too."

"Maybe we can go shopping together. I happen to know there's a tasty taco place in the food court at the mall. They're open on Sunday." His eyebrows lifted in query.

Oh. That was fast. Except . . . it wasn't. "We'll have the ham for dinner."

Aaron took her hand and laced his fingers through hers. "Let's go get Luca. Do you think he'll mind?"

"I think he'll be over the moon. Like his mom."

AARON LOOKED over as Holly came down the stairs. Everything seemed warmer. Brighter. Fuller. "He's asleep?"

She chuckled. "Oh, no. But he's in bed, and he knows he has to stay there."

"Is he okay?" They'd had lunch at the mall after church—and okay, maybe it wasn't the best choice for Easter lunch but at least the Metro DC area wasn't like a small town that shut everything down on Sundays and holidays. There was the matter of rings that needed buying. Luca hadn't minded tacos. Who did? And when they'd told him why they were looking for rings, the kid had bounced around for probably an hour straight. The conversation about Aaron being his actual father had been harder, though it had gone probably as well as it was going to go. Nine was still very young in a lot of ways. "He had an eventful day."

"He did. He's processing. I imagine we'll need follow-up conversations for a while yet. If it looks like he's struggling, I'll see about finding him someone to talk to who isn't me or you."

"A therapist?"

She nodded. "Maybe. Or maybe the pastor—the two of them get along well, and he'd be a good place to start."

"You're a good mom."

"I think I'm doing what anyone would do."

Aaron snorted. "No. I don't think so. I told him—but you could reinforce—that he's welcome to call me whenever if he wants to talk to me. About anything, not just this."

"I'll remind him." Holly snuggled next to him on the couch.

Aaron curled his arm around her, tucking her close. "I know we just got engaged, but I was wondering if you had any idea when you might want to get married. My vote is for soon."

Holly tilted her chin up and kissed his jaw. "I think we need to wait until school's out. Mid-June."

That would probably make it easier on Luca. Which mattered. And it was only two and a half months. "I can wait until June. Choose a date and tell me what I can do to help."

"Just like that?" She laughed. "Two months. No pressure."

Aaron winced. "Sorry. I guess we should talk about the kind of wedding you want. If you want a big gala, it probably takes longer to plan. You'll have to excuse me, it's my first wedding."

"Mine, too. I don't need a big to-do, but what if I call the church tomorrow and see what dates they have available? We can go from there." She wiggled a little before settling her head against his shoulder. "I'm anxious to start our life together, too."

"The contest ends in June."

She nodded.

Aaron rested his cheek against her hair and breathed in the appley scent of her shampoo. "I feel like I've already won."

EPILOGUE

Melanie Owens settled at the conference room table and glanced around. She was one of the first people there. Ryan Foster was there with Jessica Ward. And, well, well, well. Look at that sparkly ring on her left hand. Good for him—them. The little she knew of them suggested they'd make a good couple.

She sipped her coffee as Stephanie Collins entered. No ring there yet, though the rumor mill indicated that she and Christopher Ward were back together and going strong after an initial breakup. Melanie gave a slight smile. It was as if they were working from a romance novel plot outline.

She wouldn't put it past Joe Robinson. He might be the owner and founder of Robinson Enterprises, but that didn't mean he wasn't a romantic at heart. Especially not now that the love of his life from college was back and *he* was engaged. And hadn't that proposal at the company holiday party been the swooniest ever?

Movement at the door drew her eye. Ah yes, here came Aaron Powell and Holly Bell. My, oh, my. Look at the rock on her finger. That was new. Melanie chuckled.

"What's the joke?" Ian Hayes slid into a seat next to her. How had she missed his entrance? Too fixated on engagement rings to notice her partner and primary competitor in this competition come in? That wasn't good.

Melanie looked him over and bit her lip. He was good looking. Physically speaking, he ticked all the major boxes when it came to the type of guy she was usually into. They had good conversations. He challenged her and didn't mind when she fought back, but he also had a different perspective that made her think. They'd gotten to be decent enough friends since they started on this contest in January. This was the start of April. Everything would be over at the end of June. What was it going to take to win?

"What joke?"

Ian's eyebrows lifted. "You were chortling."

"I don't chortle. I can promise you, no woman chortles." Melanie shook her head. She was a writer and even she wouldn't choose that word to describe a woman. Chortling. Honestly.

"Smirking out loud? Is that better?" Ian grinned.

Melanie rolled her eyes. "If you're hoping to get on the story team, you might need to stick with your day job."

"Ouch." Ian clutched his chest before laughing. "But I guess it's fine, as I'd rather stick to marketing."

"Better you than me." She shook her head. She liked what she did—writing the storylines for video games, figuring out the choices that would branch players off into new arcs and how to tie them all together. It was the perfect job. Melanie looked around the table again at the couples who were now all seated. Was matchmaking part of Joe and Tyler's plan? Were she and Ian at a disadvantage because they were, at best, friends? Completely, one hundred percent platonic friends at that.

Tyler Shaw, Joe's right-hand man and the one technically in charge of the competition's day-to-day operation, finally came through the door. "Sorry I'm late. Before we get started, I hear some congratulations are in order."

Jessica blushed scarlet and turned to grin at Ryan at the same time as Holly held out her left hand, wiggled her fingers, and giggled. The men beamed at their women. Christopher and Stephanie exchanged a grin as well, although she wasn't sporting a rock. Maybe they really were well on their way to the same decision.

That would leave her and Ian as the only pair not engaged. Unease settled in her gut. Joe and Tyler had both mentioned—only once, but still—that they reserved the right to choose a different winner if it didn't seem like the contest results were a good fit.

Good fit.

Was it a euphemism for "good couple?"

If Joe and Tyler were matchmaking, she and Ian needed to get on board.

There was no way she'd be able to convince Ian to actually fall in love with her, but maybe she could get him to pretend.

SEE if Melanie can get Ian to play along in So You Need a Fake Relationship.

ACKNOWLEDGMENTS

I have a secret (or maybe not-so-secret) fondness for the secret baby trope. It's fun to brainstorm reasons that someone might have a baby without the other person knowing — reasons that readers won't immediately hate. And that can be tricky, too. I hope I managed the right balance between realistic and acceptable with this story, because like all authors, I'm supremely grateful that there are readers willing to take a chance on the words I've written.

I couldn't do any of this without the support of my family. My husband encourages my dreams, pretends to be interested when I'm ranting about misbehaving characters ("You're the author, why don't you just delete it and write it the way you wanted it to go?" Hahaha. If only it was that easy, honey. If only.) And generally does a bang up job of being my best friend and partner in crime no matter what life throws our way. I'm also grateful for my kids and thankful for the many hours they held off on killing each other so I could have time to write. (I won't say I had peace and quiet, because in a house of boys, that simply doesn't happen, but they did limit the number of times they needed intervention to a number under a million.)

Thanks, as always, go to my writer friends for understanding better than my hubby just how annoying it is when characters do what they want instead of what you tell them to do.

And more than anything or anyone else, thanks to Jesus. For loving me. For saving me. For putting up with me. For calling me His.

WANT A FREE BOOK?

If you enjoyed this book and would like to read another of my books for free, you can get a free e-book simply by signing up for my newsletter on my website.

OTHER BOOKS BY ELIZABETH MADDREY

So You Want to Be a Billionaire

So You Want a Second Chance

So You Love to Hate Your Boss

So You Love Your Best Friend's Sister

So You Have My Secret Baby

So You Need a Fake Relationship

So You Forgot You Love Me

Hope Ranch Series

So You Love Your Best Friend's Sister

Hope for Tomorrow

Hope for Love

Hope for Freedom

Hope for Family

Hope at Last

Peacock Hill Romance Series

A Heart Restored

A Heart Reclaimed

A Heart Realigned

A Heart Redirected

A Heart Rearranged

A Heart Reconsidered

Arcadia Valley Romance – Baxter Family Bakery Series

Loaves & Wishes

Muffins & Moonbeams

Cookies & Candlelight

Donuts & Daydreams

The 'Operation Romance' Series

Operation Mistletoe

Operation Valentine

Operation Fireworks

Operation Back-to-School

Prefer to read a box set? Find the whole series here.

The 'Taste of Romance' Series

A Splash of Substance

A Pinch of Promise

A Dash of Daring

A Handful of Hope

A Tidbit of Trust

Prefer to read a box set? Get the series in two parts! Box 1 and Box 2.

The 'Grant Us Grace' Series

Wisdom to Know

Courage to Change

Serenity to Accept

Joint Venture

Pathway to Peace

Prefer to read a box set? Grab the whole series here.

The 'Remnants' Series:

Faith Departed

Hope Deferred

Love Defined

Stand alone novellas

Kinsale Kisses: An Irish Romance

Luna Rosa (part of A Tuscan Legacy)

Non-Fiction

A Walk in the Valley: Christian encouragement for your journey through infertility

For the most recent listing of all my books, please visit my website.

ABOUT THE AUTHOR

Elizabeth Maddrey is a semi-reformed computer geek and homeschooling mother of two who lives in the suburbs of Washington D.C. When she isn't writing, Elizabeth is a voracious consumer of books. She loves to write about Christians who struggle through their lives, dealing with sin and receiving God's grace on their way to their own romantic happily ever after.

facebook.com/ElizabethMaddrey

instagram.com/ElizabethMaddrey

amazon.com/Elizabeth-Maddrey/e/BooAiiQGME

bookbub.com/authors/elizabeth-maddrey

www.ingramcontent.com/pod-product-compliance
Lightning Source LLC
Chambersburg PA
CBHW022128170626
46808CB00002B/893